If I Could Turn Back Time

MARY FRAME

She's a spectral cynic. He's a time traveler racing the clock.

Amelia Peters doesn't believe in ghosts. After outing her late paranormal investigator parents as con artists, the natural skeptic wants nothing to do with anything even supposedly spooky. But her long-held disbelief in the supernatural crumbles when she inherits a small-town cabin... and keeps bumping into a handsome specter in the night.

Shaken by the mysterious hunk's disturbing ability to vanish into thin air, Amelia is stunned to discover he's no ghost, but a traveler who has slipped through time... and is destined to die within days. When their relationship takes an intimate turn, she vows to save his skin. But altering history means confronting her own guilty secrets first.

Can they undo the mystical mayhem scaring away their happily ever after, or will the time-space continuum keep them apart forever?

Chapter One

"What if I have family?" I glance over at Bob, lounging in the passenger seat like the lazy dictator she is. She flicks her orange striped tail with annoyance.

"Can you imagine? Aunts, uncles, maybe even cousins my age."

She yawns, baring her tiny feline teeth in my direction.

"Then I could have conversations that are reciprocal instead of me talking to you, and you thinking you're better than me."

She stretches, flopping back against the seat.

"You're right. You are better than me. You might be my pet, but I am your obedient servant." I slow the truck, removing my foot from the gas as we enter town limits. "We're almost there."

I swallow, palms slick on the steering wheel. The nerves thundering through me are a direct contrast to the quaint, wholesome, all-American small town surrounding us.

The estate attorney's office is at the other end of town, according to my GPS. I gaze out the front window of the truck, one eye on the road in front of me, the other taking in downtown Mystic Falls. It's like driving through a movie set. One of those heart-warming dramedies with B-list actors, kids on bikes delivering newspapers every morning, and tree lined streets.

The brick storefronts are stacked closely together, wooden walkways running in a long line in front of them. Red and yellow trees march in a colorful procession down the street. Halloween decorations pepper windows, skeletons and mummies. The occasional witch and giant black spider perches on stretched cotton webbing.

A mountain rises in the distance, fat, fluffy clouds hanging above it in the bright blue sky.

I park behind a sleek black BMW, my ancient red pickup belching to a stop and clashing with the surroundings like a wart-covered troll in the middle of a picturesque meadow.

I take a deep breath.

Focus on the next steps. One thing at a time.

Restored Victorian-style homes line the street, all of them remodeled into businesses for a salon and spa, a coffee and tea shop, and a real estate office. A bronze placard reading *Stone & Stone* hangs on a home with blue and white trim.

"Time to get into the carrier, Bob." My voice wobbles with rising anxiety.

What if I do have family, and they hate me? After all, Mr. Stone, the attorney, wasn't surprised when I told him Dad never talked about my grandfather.

Your father and grandfather had a strained relationship, he'd said in apologetic, soothing tones.

Ha. Strained relationship. That implies there was some kind of connection. Communication. Not complete silence. There was no relationship. Dad never mentioned his family. Neither did Mom. Ever. And when I asked, I would get the brush off or they would change the subject. Maybe I should have pushed harder, but, well, it's too late now.

I glance at the clock. It's only two, and the appointment is at three. I'm early. But maybe I can get this over with and get up to the cabin before dark.

I pull the carrier from the narrow backseat of the pickup, taking a moment to glance over the boxes stuffed in the bed of the truck. They hardly shifted the entire drive from LA to Northern California. I packed everything I own—which isn't much—along with what's left of my parents' belongings, mostly notebooks and trinkets and things they collected over many years of traveling.

I'm used to being a minimalist. We moved around a lot when I was growing up and nomadic lifestyles do not lend themselves to accumulating anything but the bare necessities.

Bob meows at me a few times in protest before climbing in. "Sorry. You know it's better than the alternative."

The alternative would be leaving her in the truck. And while the weather is mild enough that it wouldn't be a safety issue, Bob goes a little berserk if I leave her in a confined space and I'm not within her line of sight. She's a tad protective.

I take just a second to glance at myself in the rearview mirror. My long dark hair is greasy and yet somehow also frizzy. My hazel eyes are puffy, outlined by gray smudges from a lack of sleep, but there's no helping it now.

Here we go.

A bell jangles overhead when I step inside.

Dark green wallpaper and mahogany trim greet me as soon as I enter the foyer. A narrow staircase on the left leads up to the second story, but the stairs are closed off with a thick burgundy rope. To the right is a closed door, to my left an open office space.

A woman with a bright and friendly smile pops out from behind a large maple desk to greet me.

She's petite and dressed in an impeccably pressed bright blue pantsuit. She's probably close to my age, mid to late twenties max. Her curly hair is pulled back, a few dark chocolate strands popping out to frame her face.

"Hello. You must be Amelia Peters."

"Yes."

"Lexi Stone." I shake her outstretched hand, hoping

my palm isn't sweaty as she gives me a firm and quick handshake. "Did you drive up from L.A. today?"

I nod. "I left this morning."

Her dark brows lift. "That's a long drive."

I shrug. "Nine hours."

Her eyes dip to the carrier in my hand and she bends down. "And who is this?"

"This is Bob."

At the sound of her name, Bob yowls.

Lexi laughs and reaches toward the crate door. "Hi, Bob."

Bob hisses and swipes fully extended claws in her direction.

"Oh, I'm so sorry." I yank the carrier away even as Lexi backs up a step. "Bob isn't great at first impressions."

But Lexi just waves me off. "I need a cat like that. Where did you get him?"

"Her. I rescued her from a trash can in Iowa when she was just a kitten."

It was the first time I really fought with my parents. Animals aren't easy to take care of when you spend your life on the road, but Bob had no one else. I couldn't leave her.

"Bob is a girl, huh? I like that." She grins. "You can bring her in here while you wait. Dad should be ready in just a few minutes."

"It's fine. I know I'm a little early." I follow Lexi into her office.

"Sit wherever you like. Would you like some coffee or something?"

"Coffee would be great." I perch on the couch across from her desk and put Bob on the seat next to me.

While she gets the coffee from a side table, I take in the space. It's mostly neat, some stacks of papers and files on the desk. A couple of framed diplomas line the wall. One photo is angled on the corner of the desk. It's a close-up selfie of Lexi with a man. Their cheeks are squished together, their mouths open in laughter, their eyes crinkled shut. It's goofy and a contrast to the professional surroundings. Funny. Lexi is pretty and she seems nice. It tracks that she would have a hot boyfriend or husband or something.

And I'm alone. All alone.

Stop being melodramatic, Amelia.

Bob grumbles next to me as she settles, like she can sense my thoughts.

I do have Bob. That's something, I guess.

But maybe it's all about to change. Maybe I do have family. Maybe they're just not here yet.

I open my mouth to ask but Lexi speaks. "Cream or sugar?"

"Uh, both. Please."

It's silent except for the faint jingle of the spoon in the ceramic mug.

My heart pounds as I clear my throat and ask the question that's been circling in my mind all day. "Are we waiting on anyone else?"

She hands me the mug and then shakes her head with a smile. "Nope. Just you. You're the sole heir."

The words drop like stones, piling in my stomach.

Other people might be happy to be the sole heir, to not have to share their inheritance. Not me. I wish this room were full of people vying for a fortune. I'd take anyone. Nefarious aunts, creepy cousins, uncles who embellish family stories and hug you just a little too long. Well, maybe not that last one.

"I mean, I guess you aren't the *sole* heir. The historical society and a representative from the church were both here the other day for their portion. But the rest is yours. Not that you need it. I heard they're making a movie from your life." She flashes a quick, bright grin. "Congratulations on all your success."

"Yeah. Thank you." I attempt to muster a pleased expression. A book deal. Movie rights. It's the dream, right? My happy act must not be convincing because Lexi's smile falters.

Ill-gotten gains. The phrase lives rent-free in my head, circling like a vulture over a carcass, periodically taking bites.

My parents were world-renowned paranormal investigators before they died. I published a story about one of their cases from when I was a kid. I'd wrote it in a moment of guilt, trying to work through my pain, not thinking anything of it beyond that. I've written hundreds of other articles about random things as a freelance writer, and not once did I have anything go viral.

Until that damn story.

The door by the entrance swings open.

"I'm sorry I can't be of more help." Mr. Stone's voice is rough with age and experience.

He has white hair, a friendly lined face, and gold-rimmed glasses. His dark suit and blue tie matches Lexi's pantsuit.

Cute.

"Your three o'clock is here, Dad," Lexi tells him.

I stand and move toward him to shake his hand.

"Ms. Peters. Thank you for making it today."

"Are you Gregory's granddaughter?" the woman standing next to him asks. She's probably about the same age as Mr. Stone, maybe early to mid-seventies. Her hair is white, pulled back into a soft bun exposing luminous pearl earrings and a matching necklace. She holds a cane in one hand, dark wood, delicately carved but sturdy and thick, the head of some kind of animal with jeweled eyes. *Old money* might as well be tattooed on her forehead.

"I guess I am."

Her eyes soften even as her smile widens. "I knew him well. My husband's family sold the cabin's property to your grandfather when your father was just a baby. Oh, I'm forgetting my manners. I'm Claire Blake."

She reaches out her hand for me to shake and her grip is as delicate as a hummingbird, a contrast to the forcefulness of Lexi and Mr. Stone.

"It's nice to meet you."

"Your grandmother was a friend as well. She's been

gone now nearly twenty years, you know, God rest her soul. If you ever want to join me for coffee and pie to hear stories of your family, my house is open."

"You definitely don't want to turn down Claire's famous strawberry rhubarb." Mr. Stone pats his stomach and grins.

"I make them from scratch using fruit from my garden."

I cling to the idea—stories of my family, making friends. It's better than the nothing I've got now. Maybe we'll start a smutty book club or something. "Thank you so much. I would really appreciate that."

One-handed, she smoothly retrieves a business card from her clutch and hands it to me. It's heavy, cream, expensive paper with her name and phone number.

"Any time, my dear." She pats my arm.

"Would you like help out to your car, Claire?" Lexi offers.

"Yes please," she says before turning back to me. "My son is waiting for me. It was a pleasure to meet you."

"You, too."

I grab Bob and then follow Mr. Stone into his office, the ambience a continuation from the entry, all masculine colors and chunky furniture.

Bookshelves take up the entire wall behind his desk, the leather-bound tomes lending everything an authentic, rich, antique vibe. Everything is pristine and yet somehow also well worn, like it has some sort of history. Multiple pictures of family sits on his desk, Lexi, and what must be his wife. A family photo features a large group of people in matching shirts like it's a reunion. People don't know how lucky they are.

I sit in a leather seat across from him and try to pay attention while he reads the details of the inheritance.

My grandfather left his main property, which was within the town's historic district, to the city. Money and most of his other assets went to the church.

My portion is a small cabin just outside of town, up an unmarked road in the woods sitting on fourteen acres.

The only stipulation is that I have to live in it for one year. It's completely paid off. I only have to cover property taxes, insurance, utilities, and general maintenance and upkeep.

"You can stay for the year?"

I nod quickly. "Yes." Hopefully longer. Hopefully forever.

So I don't have any family. So what? I've been alone for years now. Maybe this small town is where I can find my family. Establish roots. LA never felt like home. It felt like a city full of individuals who cared only about themselves and how things appeared, not how they were.

Once he's finished listing all the legal details, I sign the paperwork.

"Lexi has the directions and all the keys. She'll let you know exactly what to expect when you get up there."

"Thank you."

"There is one other thing you should be aware of."

His expression is somber. "Not because it's a problem, but because in a town this small a lot of people like to talk, and it's not always accurate."

"Okay." I brace myself. What could this be about?

"Your grandfather used the property as a rental for a short time." He pauses, his mouth turning down.

"Is someone still living there?" Or were they, and then they got evicted because of me? That's a lovely way to make a fresh start in a new place, by getting people kicked out of their homes.

"No, no, nothing like that. It's been vacant for going on three years now. Your grandfather had a hard time leasing it after the last renter—" He clears his throat, takes off his glasses, and sets them on the desk before meeting my eyes. "There's no easy way to say this, but he died there on the property."

Chapter Two

"It was difficult for Gregory to find another renter after that. You understand how people are. Considering your background, I didn't think it would be an issue. But I wanted you to hear it from me before you heard it somewhere else."

My cheeks heat. Of course it won't be a problem for me. "Thank you. I do appreciate it and I'm not concerned."

We say goodbye and he hands me a business card in case I need anything—this one not quite as lavish as Claire's—and I exit his office, Bob in hand.

In the front room, Lexi stands up behind her desk. "Let me grab the directions and everything you need for the cabin."

She picks up a folder from the corner of her desk and rifles through papers before handing me documents. "Here's the directions. The power and other utilities were restored last week. We used administrative funds from the trust to make sure it was livable and everything is in order and intact, but nothing has been cleaned inside so it's dusty. Your grandpa was having it cleaned somewhat regularly, but for the past six months or so, he was sick and, well, I have some cleaning supplies you can bring up with you. Oh, and there's a casserole my mom made."

"She didn't have to go to the trouble." My chest tightens. So what if other people in the world still have their mothers around to do such things?

Lexi waves me off. "She loves doing that stuff."

"That's really kind." I should be thankful. It's not her fault my parents are gone.

"An inspection was done last month on the roof and foundation and pipes. He didn't rent it out after the last tenant, who, well—" She cuts off, shaking her head and handing over the folder.

I take it from her. "Your dad mentioned that the last tenant passed away."

Lexi blows out a breath and blinks a few times. "Yes."

"I'm sorry, did you know them?"

"Yes." She swallows and then shakes her head. "It's fine. I mean, he died in October. On Halloween, actually, so this month isn't really *fine*, at all, but I wanted you to know, because I hope that doesn't bother you. I mean, I know with everything you've seen it might be—"

"It's okay." I assure her. "I'm used to it. And that's sort of a fallacy. Just because someone died there doesn't make it haunted. Even if it was on Halloween." I force what I hope is a comforting smile.

"Right." She exhales a breath of relief. "It wasn't anything nefarious, just a freak accident, but he was well known in the community."

"Your dad mentioned people might talk. I'm not worried about it."

The words are true, but not for the reason she thinks. The potential of a haunted cabin doesn't scare me because I know better than anyone that ghosts don't exist.

Bob brushes past me into the house, leaving delicate paw prints in the fine layer of dust covering the wood floors. With a flick of her tail, she turns down a darkened hallway on the right. I take a few steps inside as she disappears through a partially opened door like she knows exactly where she's going.

I drop my suitcase.

It's not as bad as I imagined. Driving up to the property, the first impression made my eyes bulge out of my head despite Lexi's assurances about the inspection and the property being livable. The paint is faded and chipped, the sagging front porch surely violates some safety codes, and the shutters around the windows are cockeyed and barely hanging on—a stiff wind will likely send them flying.

The interior isn't as bad. I can deal with it, my blood pressure already falling.

In front of me, the narrow entryway runs forward a few feet and then opens into a living room bright with natural light. Windows line the opposite wall with a door leading out onto a wood deck. Giant pine trees soar overhead and stretch down below, a tapestry of greens. Drawn to the landscape, I step farther into the living room. A ravine drops beyond the house, and way down below, the pine trees are dotted with the occasional bright red bush or yellow maple.

"Bob, we have a patio." I grin into the surrounding woods.

Furniture shrouded in sheets takes up most of the space around me. Creepy, but I can dig it.

"The wallpaper is . . ." ancient, faded pink and brown roses and flowers. "Antique."

One wall in the living room is almost entirely covered in crucifixes of various sizes, encircling an angelic picture of Jesus, his head tilted, a golden circle of illumination around him.

"Interesting." I wonder if last resident or my grandfather hung all of this up. Dad did know a lot about the Bible, so that sort of fits.

A flat screen hangs on another wall, a brick fireplace framing a push-button gas insert underneath it. Surprising. The flat screen and the modern fireplace make an odd contrast with the rest of the century-old home. White built-in bookshelves sits empty except for a few trinkets and an old, dusty Polaroid camera. I pick it up, leaving fingerprints in the dust, and then put it back down. Does it work? Some kind of toy or something sits on another shelf. I blow the dust off it, revealing a little gold grinning head. Strange. I put it back down, noticing a toy car on another shelf— a . . . DeLorean.

Huh.

Lexi mentioned there may be some items left behind by the last resident.

I don't have much stuff of my own to put in here, only my parents' journals and trinkets.

My attention dips down to the fireplace, excitement tripping through me. I'll be sitting in front of a crackling fire drinking tea while it snows outside in no time.

The kitchen is small but open, all white cabinets and blue tiled countertops. The appliances appear to be circa 1986 but in good shape. An old wired phone cradles in a white headset on the wall. I pick it up and there's a dial tone. "Amazing."

To the left of the living room—really, it's a continuation of the kitchen—is a small dining area with a circular pine table and four matching chairs. "Oh, Bob, our own dining room. It's like we're a real couple now."

My heart swells with something that might be pride.

I should be exhausted. I've barely slept the past few days and I woke up at four this morning to get out of

LA, but energy zips through me as I breathe in my new home along with the smell of dust and disuse.

My. New. Home.

And this isn't *ill-gotten gains*. It belonged to my family and my grandfather left it to me. I'm still shocked he even knew I existed. I wish he had reached out before he died, but that isn't something I could control.

This house, though, this I can accept.

"We have a home, Bob." The words are a whisper.

Moving quickly now, I go back to the hallway where Bob disappeared to check out the rest of the space.

It's only two bedrooms but they are decent sized, the master large enough to accommodate a queen-sized bed, dresser and vanity, with space between. There's a full bath connected to the master bedroom, too.

"The bathroom is very pink. I can learn to like pink."

It's five o'clock now. I doubt I'll get much in the way of deep cleaning done today, so it's time to focus on the essentials. There are only a couple hours of daylight left and my energy levels are going to plummet.

I unload the rest of the boxes from my car—plus the cleaning supplies and the casserole Lexi gave me, which goes into the fridge. As for the rest, there's not much. I put my parents' journals and belongings in the second bedroom where I intend to set up my office.

Leaving most of my clothes in their boxes, I place them in the master closet underneath some old coats and plastic covered who-knows-what already in there.

I hang up my extra special Cotton Candy Cat plush

robe—a present from Colleen—on a hook in the bathroom.

Bob meows, extending the yowl into something low and menacing. I follow the sound back to the closet, where Bob is smacking the old dusty clothes with her paws, punching at them like they've offended her. "Bob, no." I manage to get her claws out of the plastic and then she skitters away, running out of the bedroom down the hall somewhere.

"Crazy cat." At least the closet doesn't smell musty. Smells kind of nice actually, reminding me of Earl Grey tea, sort of spicy and orangey like bergamot. Maybe someone left those cedar blocks that keep out insects.

I uncover a sofa, love seat, and recliner in the living room, coughing into the dust filling the air.

"Bob, we have furniture."

I throw the sheets into the laundry room, where I already have the bed linens washing so I can sleep on something clean tonight.

"This couch looks comfortable." I plop down and then bounce on it, checking the springs. So it might be a little old and saggy and if you tried to sleep on it, you might die, but it's acceptable for now and the seats are wide and comfortable enough for me.

"I can picture us snuggling together, eating popcorn and kibble, binge watching *Brooklyn 99*."

I open a random door between the entry and the living room, expecting a storage closet or pantry or something, but nope. Stairs lead down into the darkness. "Every haunted house needs a basement."

The stairs are wooden, narrow, and steep. The floor and walls are solid concrete. I click on the light, a bulb flickering to life overhead as two more bulbs cast glowing circles down below.

The stairs creak and groan as I descend into an open space that spans the entirety of the house. There are a handful of droopy boxes shoved to one side. Open storage lines the walls directly in front of the stairs, a few canned goods dotting the shelves. Low-hanging beams traverse the space. I rub my arms to ward off the chill. It's colder down here, which does make it an excellent space for storing food.

A breeze tickles the hair at my nape and against my own volition, I shiver.

My parents would have loved this. All the dark corners, an elusive breeze coming from nowhere, dim lighting. The perfect foil to freak people out and then take their money.

The bulb overhead flickers, the only warning before I'm plunged into darkness.

"Well, that's not creepy."

Thankfully, I left the door open up above, and light from the living room trickles down the steps.

I force myself to walk at a normal pace back up the stairs, ignoring the looming black emptiness behind me.

I'll fix the lights later.

Creeeeeeak. Thump, thump, thump.

I shut the basement door behind me. "Bob?"

Nothing. No pitter patter of paws, no meowing, purring, or hissing and snarling. It's probably just the house settling.

Thump. Thump.

Tension slides up my spine. What is that? It's like heavy footsteps or something.

Something clatters against the linoleum, startling me. But it's just Bob, sitting on the counter in the kitchen, all innocent like she didn't just swipe the keys to the floor.

My shoulders slump as she stares at me.

"You hear that, Bob?"

She watches me for another long second and then stretches out her leg in front of her and licks it.

My shoulders relax.

If someone were in the house, she would freak out and run to attack.

It's nothing. Just as I thought.

Every house makes noises, something my parents exploited to no end. Their favorite bit was when a spirit was stuck in purgatory. The religious ones always fell for that explanation especially hard. Dad knew a lot about religion. My gaze slides over to the Jesus picture and crucifixes.

Bob hisses. She jumps to the ground, back arched, fur standing on end.

With a sudden high-pitched yowl, she bolts in the direction of the bedrooms.

I take a deep breath and then follow.

She disappears into my bedroom. I stop in the doorway.

"Bob?" The light is fading, the room dim and gray, but it's bright enough to make out the shapes of the furniture inside and the fact that it's empty. The closet door is open partway, revealing a dark and shadowed interior. Something moves. Is she back in the closet attacking the clothes?

I walk over, reach inside, and yank on the light.

She's not here. It's empty.

There is a bit of room—a space wide enough to store boxes or a body—behind the hanging clothes between the clothes and the wall. I push the garments aside, but it's empty. No Bob hiding amongst the dust bunnies. I pull the cord to turn off the bulb and then shut the door.

I'm halfway across the room when—

Creeeeeeaaak.

I spin back.

The closet door is open again

Stalking over, I open it wider, yanking on the cord. The light swings back and forth, the hanging jackets casting grotesque misshapen shadows on the walls.

There's nothing here.

I step back and eye the door hinges, the knob and doorjamb, then the floor. Over time, mother nature can cause houses to settle and heave, resulting in things going out of whack. Maybe it's not level.

I turn off the light again and then push the door closed, giving it an extra nudge for good measure and jiggling the handle to make sure it's good and shut.

This time, I make it to the hallway before I come to a total sudden halt.

Creeaaakkkkk.

Ugh. Seriously?

I walk back into the bedroom, stopping just a few feet inside the door, heart pounding.

The closet is fully open, the interior shadowed. A darker outline is silhouetted inside as if there's a man in there, just standing in the shadows.

I blink rapidly and squint. It has to be the clothes.

Then it moves.

My heart catches. Breath stutters in my throat.

Not real. Just the way they are hanging.

But it moved.

I force myself to breathe in and out slowly, keeping my eyes open and fixed on the interior of the dark closet.

Stop Amelia. You're overreacting. You were just in there, twice. No one is there.

I've been to every "haunted" house from here to Mississippi. Ghosts don't run around opening and closing doors. They don't lurk in shadows. I know there is no such thing as poltergeist or hauntings. I do, however, believe in exhaustion and the mind playing tricks on you. And squatters. Squatters are a thing. People living in basements and attics and inside the walls.

I shudder. But that's not what this is. There would have been prints in the dust.

Maybe it's something like that one house outside of Chicago that had an AM radio station playing in the walls—with no speakers. It was some kind of strange, scientifically explainable disturbance involving radio waves and metal.

Resolute, I stalk toward the closet, my eyes pinned on the shadowy figure. When I'm two steps away, the plastic-covered jackets crinkle and shuffle like they're being moved aside and the shadow—it just blinks out of existence.

I come to an abrupt halt and force my hand to reach inside the dark closet, bracing myself, for what I don't know, and then yank on the light. Then I stare.

At nothing. It's empty.

I don't know how long I stand there, heart hammering in my ears before I realize minutes have passed and I haven't so much as blinked or breathed and I'm staring at a wall and some dusty, plastic-covered clothes.

A hysterical giggle escapes. I press my hand to my mouth.

I'm losing it. I'm tired. It's been a long couple of days and I haven't slept.

If my parents could see me now, I don't know if they'd be horrified or thrilled.

Chapter Three

My phone rings and I almost jump out of my skin. I force myself to take a few deep breaths before I answer.

I don't have to read the caller ID to know who it is. No one else calls me.

"Hey, Colleen." I walk out of the bedroom, needing to get away from the closet.

"How are you settling in?" Colleen is a five-foot-nothing blonde powerhouse, a strange mixture of Barbie, cheerleader, and stone-cold ball buster.

"Great. It's perfect. Quiet. I'm surrounded by trees. The nearest neighbor is about a half mile away down at the bottom of the hill. But I'm only a ten-minute drive to town. And there's an office."

"That is great! You can work on the book."

My responding silence goes on a little too long. "I've got some words down." Like twenty pages of garbage that hopefully will never see the light of day or be read by any actual human beings ever.

"That's great!" Her response is overly exuberant. "I know you can do this."

Apprehension surges through me. What if I can't?

I sit on the couch, leaning my head back and staring up at the ceiling. *Can't* isn't an option. I have to. I signed a contract selling book and film rights and received an advance for both. But I don't want the money. I went along with it because how could I refuse? Only a crazy person would say no.

Sign me up for Bedlam.

Naturally, Colleen has been pushing me to get it done. It's her job. I don't want to let her down. Not to mention my publisher, and now the film production company . . .

But putting words on the page, especially these words, is like pushing an elephant up a steep hill.

"So, this house, is it haunted?" Her tone is hushed but excited.

The framed picture of Jesus on the wall gazes down on me, his expression serene, the halo of various crucifixes too dusty to glint in the wan light. I give up counting after 14. Even if it is haunted, I'm probably safe from demons. This Jesus isn't a fire and brimstone type, he's more of the forgiving type—even if I don't deserve the compassion.

"No way of knowing yet . . ." I don't have to tell her, but I want her to have hope or something—I want to make her happy. "But the estate lawyer did say the last resident died here. I don't know. It's too soon to tell."

"Really?" She breathes out the word, drawn out and excited. "Amazing. That's incredibly lucky. We can only hope."

I cringe. There is nothing lucky about it.

"Listen, Amelia, don't stress on it, okay? You've been through a lot and if you need to take time to rest and relax, then you should absolutely do it. Nothing is worth your health and sanity. Make sure you're taking care of yourself, okay?"

I know we work together and our relationship is business, but no one has ever bothered to show any kind of concern about me since my parents died. Something expands in my chest, the idea that someone else cares, not about what I can do for them, but for me. Even if it's just a little bit.

A door slams in the background. "I gotta run. My kids just got home." Voices and laughter clamor from a distance. Colleen calls out, "Be right there!"

Then there's the murmur of a deep masculine voice, speaking in an amused cadence. "Your biggest kid is also home."

Colleen chuckles, the sound muted, like she's covering the mouthpiece. "I'll talk to you later this week, okay?"

"Yeah. Bye."

We hang up, the boisterous sounds of life cutting off.

The ensuing silence is absolute, and yet somehow deafening.

Bob yowls from the kitchen, meowing like the world is ending and she's being murdered.

"I'm coming."

I may not have love, family, friends, or anything, really, but I have Bob. Bob loves me. And Lexi gave me food for dinner. That's care and concern, even if it's just a small-town thing people do for strangers they don't intend to speak to ever again or be more than acquaintances with.

I take the dish out of the fridge and turn on the oven.

While I'm waiting, I feed Bob, setting her dish on the floor.

Lexi's really nice. Maybe we can be friends. I've never had real friends.

The four-person dining set mocks me with its empty chairs. Even if I include myself at the table, I don't have enough friends or family to fill it up. Is it possible to have relationships that last longer than a carton of milk when I have to lie to everyone about my entire life?

My body is weighted down, heavy with sleep. And yet I'm awake enough to be aware of my surroundings. I'm in bed in my cabin with Bob's slight weight pressing on my legs. Everything is as it should be, but at the same time, it's all wrong. Even behind my closed eyelids, the world is smothered in a muted, colorless haze.

A heavy arm rests around my waist, like it belongs there. Heat runs along the length of my back.

I should be freaked out. Someone is in bed with me, spooning me. This isn't normal, and yet it is. I'm so warm. Me and my dream man lying together in the darkness, our breathing in sync.

Something shifts. There's a pulse, an awareness breaking through the fog. His arm tightens, just the slightest movement, but it's like a signal that provokes action.

My back arches, pressing myself back into him in a slow, irresistible roll. The hard length his erection sears my back. A gentle breath puffs against my ear. I should be terrified. Scared.

But I've been here before.

His breath catches, the sound as familiar as my own inhale and exhale. Soft lips brush the back of my neck, trailing down to the juncture where my shoulder begins.

He smells amazing. Bergamot, sandalwood, and sleepy, sexy man.

The hand around my waist slides up to cup my breast. The fingers are soft, knowing, exerting exactly the right pressure.

I shift, restless, and the hand slides down between my legs. Air hisses through teeth behind me as he slips his fingers under the waist of my pajama pants.

I'm already slick with desire and so turned on I

might break apart at a single touch. His palm presses against the bundle of nerves, his fingers sliding through my folds. Both of us breathing heavier, he thrusts against me from behind, helplessly, almost like he can't control the movement. His hand moves faster against me, a finger slipping inside. I push back, in time with his movements, and then like the snap of a band, rapture blasts through me.

A grunt behind me, breath blowing over the back of my neck that cuts off mid exhale, like a candle being snuffed out.

The heat disappears.

Coldness intrudes.

He's gone. Like he was never even there.

All at once, I'm bereft, and the colorless world I've been cocooned in dissolves into regular gray-blue darkness.

Still only half awake, I snuggle further into the comforter, only one thought lingering in the post-orgasm bliss and subsequent abrupt disappearance of my dream man.

Come back.

Chapter Four

Knock, knock, knock.

Groaning, I roll over and tug the pillow over my head.

"Yoooowwwl."

"Bob, shut up."

She jumps on my back, kneading her paws into me.

Knock, knock, knock.

I flop over, Bob jumping away before she can be squished while I fumble for my cell phone plugged in on in the nightstand. "No more ghosts."

I stare at the time, blinking at the numbers. They can't be real. It's after ten. I haven't slept this late in years.

Must have been that awesome sex dream. I glance over at the empty side of the bed, rubbing at a lingering hollowness that throbs underneath my breastbone. How can I miss someone that doesn't exist?

I didn't even see his face. Am I that desperate? Apparently, since I orgasmed in my sleep.

Do grown-ass women have wet dreams? Is that a thing?

I blink in the sun-drenched room. What happened last night?

That was some wild dream. I want to fall back into it.

It was more than just the physical aspect. It was like the person in bed knew me. Loved me. Accepted me. Such an impossibility.

I flop back into the pillow and turn my head into it. The faint scent of bergamot lingers. It smells so good. I breathe it in deeper, trying to remember . . . wait. How can my pillow still smell from a dream?

Knock, knock, knock.

Crap. I heave back up into a sitting position. Someone's here.

Scrambling out of bed, I race to the door. "Coming!" How long have they been waiting?

I swing it open and come face to face with a tall, dark, and impeccably dressed man standing on my porch.

I blink at him, mouth dropping open.

He's holding a thick ivory vase. A green stem protrudes from its depths, topped with delicate, bright blue blossoms. Some kind of fancy orchid.

His eyes drop down my body.

"Uh." Shit. I'm wearing an oversized T-shirt with a

hole in the side and a curry stain on the front. And that's it. Just the T-shirt and panties hidden somewhere underneath the stained hem.

"Can I help you?" My voice is pitched at a level only animals can hear.

"Hello." His smile is wide and bright and looks like a lot of expensive dental work. I take the rest of him in. Dark hair, recently trimmed. Chiseled features. Fancy watch. Perfectly pressed pants. Not a hair out of place or a flaw in sight. He's handsome enough. He oozes an ingrained sense of entitlement only people with money can truly pull off. Kind of reminds me of everything I hated in LA.

"You must be Amelia," he continues. "I'm Preston Blake. You met my mother yesterday, Claire Blake. She asked me to stop by and welcome you to town. And to bring you this." The smile flashes again, blinding me. "It's a rare blue orchid."

Called it. "Oh. Thank you." I take the heavy and awkward potted flower and hold it against my side like it's a toddler.

"Nice to meet you. Sorry I'm not, um." I glance behind me into the house.

With a battle cry worthy of a feral wildcat, Bob leaps out and latches onto Preston's leg—gripping around his calf with both her paws and hindlegs. She bites and warbles like the little psycho she is, digging in with her claws and gnawing at his pants like he's a fried chicken drumstick.

"Bob, stop. I'm so sorry." I put the plant down on the ground, squatting next to Preston, grabbing Bob around the waist and tugging, but she doesn't letting go.

Mortification swamps me.

Every time I pull her back, the pants come with her, stuck in her claws.

Preston shakes his leg, attempting to get her off, but only succeeds in kicking me in the side with one shiny leather shoe.

She lets out a growl. My face is on fire. "I'm not sure what's gotten into her."

I know what's gotten into her. She's a total asshole. And she hates everyone, but especially men. The last time I had a date stay the night, he left with a dozen scratches, and not from exuberant sex.

Once I finally get her claws unstuck from his pants, I back into the house, holding Bob around her waist. She slumps in my arms, playing dead since she knows she's in trouble.

Preston's smile has turned forced. He lets out a chuckle laced with irritation. "That's a, uh, really good guard pet you have there."

"She's very protective." Maybe it would be easier to have friends if Bob didn't attempt to kill everyone I meet.

"Right. Well. Let me give you my card." He whisks a small square from somewhere in his coat pocket Band hands it to me. Bob comes to life, swiping at his outstretched fingers.

I shove down the urge to burst into laughter, shifting Bob in my arms to hold her farther away and take the proffered card from him.

It's exactly like his mother's except his card is black with white print while hers was all white with black print.

"If you need anything, give me a call. I grew up here so I can show you around." Another forced smile.

"Thank you. That's very kind."

"And if you have any issues with the cabin, I can help." He steps down the porch steps, turning to flash me another megawatt smile.

"You . . . can?" Does he think it's haunted? My mind flashes back to the figure in the closet.

"I own a contracting company."

"Oh. You do home renovations?" I relax. "I think I just need to get it painted. Eventually."

"I also own a real estate company, so if you decide to sell, I can help with that, too."

"I can't sell for at least a year."

"Ah." He nods in understanding.

I shift Bob in my arms. Would it be rude to just shut the door now? "Well I have to, um, get dressed, but thank you for the plant, uh, flower thing. And sorry about Bob."

"No problem." He winks. "I'm sure I'll be hearing from you."

What? *No.* "Right. Yeah. Bye."

I shut the door, then peer through the peep hole. Of course he drives a BMW. I wait until he's disappeared, driving down the gravel drive and kicking up dust as he goes.

"I guess I should be thankful he doesn't want me to pay to fix his suit," I tell Bob.

After he's gone, I put some pants on and get to work. Today will be cleaning, shopping, and setting up the house. Maybe even getting some writing done if there's time.

It's my first full day in my new hometown and I can't wait to check it out. Maybe meet someone who isn't rich and awkward.

"Bob. This could be the start of something wonderful."

<hr>

"Go back to LA, freak!"

The words are shouted out of the open window of a giant black pick-up truck as I'm walking into the supermarket.

I glance around. A woman is placing grocery bags in her trunk while her toddler bangs on the handle of a cart with some kind of blue plastic toy. An elderly couple totters through the front doors, just about to disappear inside. Otherwise, the lot is empty. Except for me.

But they couldn't have been talking to me. Right? I

just got here. I've only met like four people in this whole town.

The grocery store is larger than I expected for a small town, the building farmhouse style. I grab pasta, fruit, veggies, wine, tea, all the essentials. I smile at the few people I pass, but most of them won't meet my eyes. Aren't people in small towns supposed to be all kind and friendly to everyone?

Maybe it's an off day.

Maybe they fear me because I'm a stranger. Or they think I'm a tourist. Not really tourist season, though.

A friendly voice finally finds me as I stand in the one and only checkout line.

"Amelia, hey."

I spin around.

It's Lexi. She's casual today in frayed jean shorts and a white crop top that cinches at her waist. Her hair is pulled back in a messy ponytail, curls escaping.

"Oh, hi. Tell your mom I said thank you again for the casserole. It was delicious."

She beams. "I'm so glad you liked it. How are you settling in?"

"Oh, fine, fine. It's really good."

The line moves forward and I stack my items onto the conveyor belt.

The cashier is a middle-aged woman in a red flannel and white apron with wide cheeks and a scowl. She slams my carrots into one of the bags. Then my cookies. Then my wine.

I wince. "I'm sorry, can I . . . help?" Is there something I'm supposed to be doing here? Is this one of those self-bag places and I've committed some terrible faux pas since I didn't immediately pony up? Should I have brought recyclable bags?

"Carol, what the hell?" Lexi asks.

Carol glares at me. Then at Lexi.

"I know who she is." She points a box of tampons at me, her lip curling in disgust.

Heat creeps up my face. Oh, no. Not here. This is like middle school all over again.

Lexi snorts. "You shouldn't listen to rumors. Not very Christian of you, and I think Pastor Mike would agree."

Carol aims her death stare in Lexi's direction.

"Rumors?" My voice is a squeak.

I just got here yesterday and there are already rumors?

Lexi waves a dismissive hand. "Don't worry about it." Then she raises her voice and scowls at Carol. "Only people with no sense listen to old gossip about people they know nothing about."

Carol's glare ticks up a couple notches from hatred to pure revulsion.

It doesn't deter Lexi, though. "Yeah, Carol, I'm talking about you, so go ahead and snarl."

"Oh. I'm . . . I'm sorry." I don't know what else to do. You'd think I'd know how to respond to this by now, but I don't. I can't. I wanted Mystic Falls to be different.

I hand over my debit card, paying in silence before putting the bags in the cart.

I finish paying and then, in a daze, race out the exit before someone else says something terrible.

Crap. I stop halfway through the parking lot. I didn't even say good bye to Lexi. Great. Now she'll hate me, too.

I'm loading the back of the truck with my bags when Lexi passes me in the parking lot, cart jangling over the pocked asphalt.

"Sorry about that. Carol's harmless. She's bored and repeating stupid rumors. People in this town have nothing better to do than find something or someone to complain about."

"What rumors could possibly be going around? Is it because of my parents?"

She grimaces. "Yeah. Sort of. Word got out faster than I thought about you inheriting the cabin. Since Dad and I legally have to keep our mouths shut about everything, you can rest assured it wasn't us. But someone saw you come into town and knows who you are, and I guess people are worried about you bringing your Hollywood entourage. Next thing you know there's a Starbucks on every corner and three Walmarts and people think it's the end of life as we know it."

"But I don't have an entourage." I don't have anyone. "I'm just a writer. No one cares about writers." One viral article does not make me Stephen King.

She winces and then shrugs. "I think it's more than

that. Your family has lived in this area forever. Even though your dad left thirty years ago, people have long memories in small towns, and the stories get taller and taller with each repetition. Some people might be lukewarm about him and what happened with your grandad. Some people think he was the devil incarnate for the things he did and said he saw. And Paul left. Gregory stayed. Most people took his side because it's the one they heard the most and they blamed your dad for his mother's death."

"Why?"

"She was never the same after he left and never really recovered. Some people think she died of a broken heart."

"But I had nothing to do with any of that. I wasn't even born yet."

She shrugs. "Guilt by association? If it helps, some might decide you're good since Gregory left the property to you. He wouldn't have done so if he thought you were truly evil. But then again, he might have felt responsible since your dad died before they could reconcile. Death has a way of leaving behind a trail of guilt."

I close the tailgate. "I appreciate you telling me all of this. And being nice to me. Why are you being so nice to me?"

She glances away and then back to meet my eyes. "I lost my best friend." She shrugs. "I could use more friends. And I think that you could use a friend, too."

I nod. "I really could." If only she knew.

"Everyone will warm up once they stop being dumb-asses and get to know you."

"Thank you for sticking up for me back there."

She waves me off. "It's no problem."

I glance behind me at the truck, about to say good-bye, but something smeared on the windshield snags my attention.

"Hang on," I murmur, distracted. "What is . . .?" I round the truck to get closer. There's something spread all over the windshield and the driver's side door. I reach out to touch it but it's already drying, and there's little white pieces of—I gasp. "Someone egged my truck."

"Oh no." Lexi is right behind me. "Hold on, I have some napkins in my car. We should get off what we can before it dries and damages the paint." She glances over the old, worn truck. "Not that you might actually worry about that."

It's old and cracked in spots anyway, but still. This was Dad's truck.

I stand there, staring at the egg-splattered door, and wonder if my life will ever change.

Lexi returns with some napkins and wet naps and helps me clean it off as much as possible.

Once we're done, she takes all the trash to throw away and then asks, "Hey, do you want to get some drinks or something Saturday night at Mystic Bar? Once people see you aren't practicing voodoo or wearing all black with upside-down crosses and demon symbols tattooed on your neck, maybe they'll calm down."

I swallow. She's right. They might hate me now, but I can change their mind. Maybe. And at least I'll have one friend. If that's all I get, I'll take it. "Yeah. That sounds good."

<h1 style="text-align:center">Chapter Five</h1>

Replacing the bulbs in the basement is not as bad as I thought it would be. After a trip to the hardware store for a high-powered flashlight, I can illuminate the space while I work.

After getting the first bulb changed, I step off the stool and bend over to pick up the flashlight, something small and shiny winking at me from against the wall as it glitters in the light.

Keeping the flashlight trained on the shimmering object, I pick it up and place it in my palm, examining it under the light.

It's a red gemstone, marquise shaped and at least three carats. It's probably fake. Maybe it belonged to my grandmother.

Thump, thump, thump.

I glance up, pointing the light overhead as if it will

beam through the ceiling and straight into the upper floor.

Not this again.

I shove the gemstone into the pocket of my jeans and head upstairs.

A door opens and then slams shut from the direction of my bedroom.

Okay. Hold up now. That wasn't like a house settling noise. I don't think Bob could manage slamming a door, but I can't put it entirely past her.

I stalk in the direction of the sound. That demon cat better not be attacking those coats again, as I want to donate them—

Halting in the doorway, I open my mouth to scream but nothing emerges. Not even a croak.

There's a man in my bedroom.

The sun setting has made the room almost entirely dark, except for the light spilling from the closet and illuminating his form. His back is to me, and he's resting his arms on the doorframe facing the interior, like he's searching for something inside.

He wears a white button up dress shirt and black slacks, a dark tie loose around his neck as if he's been tugging on it.

The pose highlights the muscles in his back, his dark hair, broad shoulders, and tapered waist.

From this angle, I can just make out the corner of a jaw peppered with the shadow of a beard. Even from fifteen feet away, he's . . . *hot.*

Are intruders supposed to be good looking? Ted Bundy was charming and handsome but in photos he mostly resembles a demon.

What in the hell? Why is he here and how did he get in undetected? Where's Bob?

My thoughts race.

Wait. What if it's townies, those egging bastards, trying to scare me and run me out of town?

I grind my teeth. How dare they? First my truck and now this? They can't scare me away. I know exactly how to deal with unwanted intruders. You scare them right back.

The man shifts in my direction. With a couple steps, I move back and to the side, out of sight, leaning back against the wall next to the bedroom door and trying to slow my breathing through my racing heart.

"Is someone there?" he calls.

Ha. Like he doesn't know. He's going to regret breaking into my house and trying to freak me out. You can't creep a creeper.

His footsteps approach, squeaking on the hardwood floors.

With trembling fingers, I tug my long hair over my face, covering most of my features, dipping my head, hunching my back in my best impersonation of a demon-possessed orphan who just crawled out of a well. I stand as still as I can. Waiting. Listening. Focusing on slowing my breath. If this is going to work, it has to be convincing.

The footsteps come to an abrupt halt.

"Holy hell." He jumps back, stumbling into the wall, his arms lifting in front of him in a defensive motion.

Pushing down my own instinct to flee, I open my mouth and attempt creepy moaning noises, but nerves impact my performance and the moan is more like a breathy sigh. I click my tongue instead and shuffle toward him.

He doesn't move, which makes me wonder if he'll flee or if this whole thing will backfire if he attacks.

I'm bracing myself for the latter when his shoulders shake and then he's . . . he's laughing?

I push my hair aside to be sure, and yes. He's slumped in the doorway, wiping his eyes and holding his stomach in mirth.

"This is great. Did Lexi put you up to this?" He chuckles. "Lexi!" he shouts. "Where are you? Did you put a camera in here? I told you, you can't one-up my pranks. I knew I shouldn't have told her about last night."

Lexi? Last night? What?

I stand up straight and push my hair out of my face. "Lexi isn't here. Who are you?"

He blinks at me, giving me a good look at his face.

It's too dim to really make out the exact color of his eyes, probably just brown or something equally boring, but he does not have Ted Bundy–dead eyes. He has heavy-lidded, sexy eyes offset by thick brows.

Some intrinsic part of me wakes up and says, "Oh, it's you," because he's. . . familiar.

His hands drop as he takes me in and then nods in approval. "That was pretty good. You scared the crap out of me, lady." A crease forms between his brows. "How did you get in here? When did Lexi let you in?"

"What are you talking about? I live here. I've been here all day. Who are you?"

His lips purse and he smiles. My eyes flick to his mouth, which is full and pouty and makes me think of what he can do with those lips and the fact that there's a bed only a few feet away and oh my gosh I need to get laid.

Stop being attracted to the intruder.

I don't think he's going to murder me considering I just scared the crap out of him and his initial reaction was to back away instead of going on the offense.

He doesn't seem angry or violent. He's . . . smiling. Amused.

His eyes slide over me and he blinks, shaking his head before meeting my gaze again. "Is she paying you? Whatever it is, I'll double it if you tell me when she let you in. I just saw her at the funeral and there's no way she beat me here first—unless, did she give you a key?" He rubs his bristled chin. "No. She knows better than to give some stranger keys to my house." He moves in my direction. "Who are you?"

I instinctively step back. "What? Your house?" My voice is a high-pitched squeak.

He's still walking toward me. I make it into the entry and then hold up a hand, alarm returning as he approaches. "Don't come any closer."

He stops. His head tilts, eyes roaming over my face, taking in my features. His brows lower. "Do I know you?"

"No. Now get out of my house." My hands shakes as I clench them at my sides.

He doesn't move. We stare at each other in confused silence.

"This isn't your house," he says.

"Are you a squatter?"

He laughs, brows lifting with surprise. "Do I look like a squatter?"

I mean, there could be squatters who are also mega super hotties in rumpled suits with lean muscular shoulders and trim waists. "You're halfway undressed." I point at his outfit.

He shrugs and crosses his arms over his chest, his eyes dropping, cheeks going pink. "I was about to get in the shower."

Is he embarrassed? It's kind of cute. *Stop it Amelia, he's an intruder, not a potential love interest.* "It's my shower."

"That's weird since I live here."

"No. *I* live here." I point to the front door. "And *you* need to leave."

He shakes his head and then smiles again, unconcerned. He leans against the doorjamb, all smooth male amusement. "We can go back and forth all night like this, but the short of it is, I live here, and I'm not going anywhere."

"Fine. Then I'm calling the cops."

"Not a problem. Jimmy can straighten this all out and I'm sure he'd love to hear all about Lexi's lame attempt to prank me."

"Who's Jimmy?"

He steps closer and my heart accelerates but then he turns, heading toward the kitchen. Okay, so he knows where the phone is, but that doesn't prove anything.

I follow after him, ready to argue more, but when I reach the kitchen, he's gone.

I stop in the center of the room, spinning in a circle like he might magically appear at any moment from behind a . . . coffee pot or something. What the hell?

"Hello?" I didn't get his name. "Intruder man? Where did you go?" It's not that big of a space. There aren't many places he could hide.

The floor creaks behind me and I spin around.

Bob trots toward me, rubbing against my leg before jumping up onto the counter.

"Where were you when we had an intruder?" She stares at me. Bob always protects me. Always hears everything with her animal instincts and goes into attack mode on every male within a mile radius. What the heck?

I open the door to the back patio and glance around. Nothing. There's no way he could have made it out here without me seeing, but I have to check. The trees are dark and barren and still, not even a faint breeze to make them twitch, silent sentries confirming no one has been here.

I stalk back down the hall to the bedrooms. Empty. I check the bathrooms and the closets and then circle back to the kitchen.

Then, finally, the basement. No one else is here.

He's gone.

"This isn't funny," I call out. Where did he go? My breath comes out in rapid spurts. Do I really think this is this some kind of prank? Townies trying to scare me away? Did he keep mentioning Lexi because they know she's being kind to me and they're trying to make me think she's a part of this to further alienate me?

I take a deep breath and let it out. Have I completely cracked?

Another thought niggles in my mind, impossible to ignore. What if this place is actually haunted? There was a man who died here . . .

No. It can't be.

That wasn't a ghost. It was a real, talking, breathing, *living* person.

I sit at the dining table, the darkening forest beyond the window blurring with my thoughts.

Think logically. I know this con better than anyone. Are people in town trying to trick me? Is this the next step after egging my car? Sort of a sharp escalation, but maybe.

If that's the case, they've messed with the wrong fake ghost hunter.

I have little choice. I need a record just in case this guy becomes a real problem.

"I'm calling the police," I yell.

But no one responds.

"I've checked everywhere and can't find any evidence of forced entry. Did you lock your door?"

"I'm sure I did." Is it possible to pass out from sheer embarrassment?

The officer can't be more than twenty-two. Not that I'm much older, but still. He's young and baby faced—if that baby was cranky as hell because he hasn't smiled once. I should be grateful he's forgoing any platitudes, but I'm pretty sure he thinks I'm an idiot.

He jots in his notebook, frowning down at the words after he scribbles.

I'm sitting at the dining table, my hands gripping a mug of tea while he stands between the living and dining rooms.

Bob's plaintive meows occasionally disrupt our conversation. She attacked the cop as soon as he came in the door and I had to lock her in the back bedroom—after he searched it for evidence of my intruder.

"There's no sign of forced entry," he says for the third time.

My jaw clenches.

"Will you describe the man you saw again?" His eyes lift to mine.

I take a sip of my tea. "His hair was dark. He definitely has brown hair." I shut my eyes and try to come up with better adjectives than sexy, smirky suit man. "Dark eyes, too. He was about six feet tall, maybe a couple inches above that. Probably midtwenties. Well built." My face heats. "I mean, he looked like—he looked like he worked out," I manage to get out.

His brows are furrowed as he regards me for a few quiet seconds.

His two-way radio sputters and crackles as a female voice says, "Unit one, please check in."

"Excuse me." He picks up the radio and walks out onto the patio, shutting the door behind him.

He paces outside, his voice an incoherent murmur.

No problem. I'll just be in here by myself, questioning my own sanity.

I'm sure I'm reading too much into this. He hasn't been unkind. He inspected the house thoroughly, checked the doors and windows for evidence of a break in, and asked me a few questions about what happened and where I saw the intruder. I've given him descriptions twice now. He's been attentive and serious, but it's hard to tell what he's really thinking. Does he think I'm just some crazy lady? Is he telling the dispatcher about this? Are they having a good laugh at my expense?

As if to punctuate my mortification, Bob yowls like she's dying.

The patio door opens. "Yep. Copy that."

He comes back inside, slipping the radio onto his belt. "Can I ask you another question, ma'am?"

My brows shoot up in surprise. "Of course." Ma'am? Really?

"Is this some kind of prank?"

My jaw drops. "Excuse me?"

"Listen, everyone knows who you are."

My hands clench around my mug. "What do you mean?"

He sighs. "I know you're a big-shot writer. Is this some kind of publicity stunt for your book?"

"I'm really not a big shot, and it isn't about that, I swear."

His head tilts, one brow lifting. "Isn't there, like, a movie coming out based on your life? A horror movie?"

My response is interspersed with a lot of sputtering. "I mean, there is, but that's not what this is about. I'm not lying. I'm not making this up. Someone was in my house, I swear it."

His lips thin. "Did someone tell you about the man who used to live here?"

"Who? Oh." I shake my head. "No. I mean, yes. Lexi and Mr. Stone mentioned the last person who lived here died but nothing about him."

He nods and then sighs. "His name was Grey. Greyson Holmes. He had dark hair. He was a little over six feet tall. He was captain of the swim team and went to college on a swimming scholarship. So . . . in shape and well built."

Chills race down my spine, goose bumps erupting all over my arms and neck. I shake my head. "I-I-I didn't know all that. I didn't know who he was or what he looked like. I swear it."

He shifts his feet, hands on his belt. Silence stretches for a minute, but his face softens a hair. "You said you met Lexi and Mr. Stone. I presume you went and signed papers yesterday at their office?"

I blink at the abrupt change of conversation. What does that have to do with anything? "Yes?"

"Lexi and Grey were best friends since grade school. She has a large picture on her desk of the two of them together. Did you see it?"

My mouth drops open, my mind conjuring the photo of Lexi with what I thought was her boyfriend or something.

"Oh." I mean, it could be the same person. Not that I would have recognized him from a photo I saw only at a distance. And he was grinning and squishing his face against Lexi's, but . . . what if that's why he was familiar?

So why am I seeing a dead guy in my house? And how can I explain it to this officer who thinks, at worst, I'm making it all up for attention or, at best, I have an overactive subconscious that makes me hallucinate?

I shut my eyes in defeat.

He squats down next to my chair. "Listen, it's not a

big deal. No need to get upset or anything. If you want, we can just drop the whole thing. I don't need to do a bunch of paperwork or file a report. No one needs to know what happened here, okay? We can all move on and the rest of the town will never know."

My face is hot. He's giving me an out, a way to avoid total and complete hatred from the rest of the town—people who already hate me. What am I going to do, insist he file a report like the asshole they all think I am? And if my initial suspicions are correct, if this is something as simple as townies trying to embarrass me or scare me away, this cop might be in on the ruse. Filing a report would just make things worse.

"Yeah." I nod. "Sure. That's fine. I'm sorry to waste your time."

He nods and stands. I walk him to the door. "No worries," he reassures me when he's out on the front porch. "Jimmy's cool about stuff like this. He's really chill and isn't a stickler for paperwork. He's old-school, you know?"

"Jimmy?"

"He's been the sheriff here for twenty years."

We say our goodbyes and then I shut the door, peering through the peephole as he gets into his cruiser and drives away.

I blow out a breath and rest my forehead against the door. The urge to bang it against the hard wood is almost overpowering.

I don't want to be the girl who cried ghost.

Ghosts don't run around talking to people. They don't linger. It goes against everything I was taught by my parents.

I need more sleep, clearly.

But I can't ignore the other thing.

Jimmy. He said Jimmy would straighten things out. The ghost did. Dammit. He wasn't a ghost.

But he knew the name of the sheriff. Did I already know the name of the sheriff? Maybe it *was* my subconscious, a name I heard somewhere else and didn't realize I'd heard. But also, he kept referring to Lexi like she is his friend, and she told me her friend had died here.

I'm not sure what to believe anymore.

Is this house haunted or am I?

Chapter Six

"So, I hear you had an interesting night."

I stifle a groan. "You heard about that? The police officer told me to not file a report so it wouldn't get out."

Is she pissed? What if she thinks I'm using the memory of her dead friend for notoriety? I might lose the only sort of friend I have before we even get to know each other's middle names.

But she's not angry or yelling. She's smiling, twisted around on the barstool to face me, wearing a dressy black tank and jeans. She picks up the purse lying on the chair next to her and motions for me to sit. "Don't blame baby Drew, he hasn't said anything or spilled any details, despite everyone badgering him about it. Mrs. Jenkins, who lives at the bottom of your hill, saw him driving up to your place with his lights on, and then Nancy in dispatch accidently let it slip to Bill at the coffee shop. Can't keep secrets in a town this size, I'm sorry to say."

I sigh and slide onto the chair next to her. "Should I expect more eggs?"

"Maybe you'll get an upgrade to flaming poop on your porch."

I wince.

She grins, then tilts her head toward the bar. "Drink?"

"Yes. All of them. Please." I don't know what to order. Despite the martini glass Lexi lifts to her lips, this doesn't strike me as the kind of place that would serve a Manhattan.

My eyes drift over the bar where a row of middle-aged men in flannels watch the football game on TV, the sound low. A group of five or six teenagers congregate around two pool tables in the rear next to an old juke box. Tables litter the middle of the space, but most of them are empty. Only one younger couple and a family of four eating dinner occupy the space. Framed football jerseys are the main décor, along with a few fake jack-o-lanterns in the front windows.

She lifts her martini glass "Want to start with one of these?"

"Sounds good."

She motions to the bartender, a tall woman in all black with short cropped dark hair who immediately makes her way over.

Lexi motions to the woman. "Jamison, this is Amelia. Amelia, Jamison."

Jamison nods in my direction. "Heard you moved into the old Peters place." Her voice is low and smoky.

"Yes. That's me." I give Lexi a side-eye but she just grins. "Nice to meet you."

Lexi holds up her martini. "Can you get my friend here one of these?"

"Sure." Jamison leans over the bar, her cheek next to Lexi's and lowers her voice, but the exchange is still audible. "You'll wait for me later?"

"What time are you off?"

Jamison pulls back. "Eleven."

Lexi nods and takes a delicate sip of the martini in her hand. "I can manage that."

The bartender turns away and makes my drink, throwing the occasional heated glance at Lexi.

"Is Jamison your girlfriend?" I ask.

"One of them." She grins at Jamison and then turns to me. "So, you want to talk about what happened last night?"

I blow out a breath. Not really.

I also do not want to tell her how I spent most of the day scouring the property more thoroughly than the night before, and with fresh, not so panicked eyes.

I won't mention how I tapped on walls checking for hollow spaces, then searched the attic, a small, dusty, unlivable space full of insulation.

I walked around the outside of the property, ascertaining if there were gaps in the architecture.

I'll avoid talking about the creepy basement since her

friend apparently died there, but there was nothing to see anyway. No one was there.

I also will not mention that I may have had another sexy dream last night.

Either way, an explanation would be nice. All I know is that I saw a man and he may or may not resemble Lexi's best friend, who is dead.

If he faked his own death, or if he's some kind of squatter trying to make me look like an attention whore for the townies, he's somehow been living there without disturbing anything. There were no footsteps in the dust. No fingerprints anywhere.

Maybe I can get some answers from Lexi. Which is why I have to tell her some of the truth, as much as it pains me. But she knows who my parents were. It's not going to be remarkable that I've seen a "ghost."

But what if she thinks I'm desecrating his memory like everyone else?

She's waiting for me to answer. Her eyes are interested, not accusing. And what are my options, anyway? How else am I going to figure out what is going on?

"I did see someone in the cabin." My voice is robotic. I clear my throat.

Her brows lift.

I blow out a breath. "And you told me," I wave a hand, "you said someone died there."

"I did." She leans forward, lowering her voice. "You know, my friend who lived there, he told me he saw something in that house, too."

I sit back. "He did?"

She nods. "What did you see?"

"I saw . . . a man."

Her face falls a little.

"What did he see?"

She shrugs. "He said he saw a person. He also said he kept losing things. Like items would disappear, but then a few seconds later, it would be back where he left it. It really freaked him out."

I rub my head. He saw a person? "What did the person look like?"

"He never really said. If I remember correctly, he didn't get a good look. It was dark, and it happened quickly. And he only mentioned it once. But I do remember it was the month he died. It's one of the reasons I've been looking more into his death."

Wait. What? "I thought you said it was an accident."

"That's what everyone thinks but . . ." She glances around and shakes her head. "Tell me more about what happened last night."

"Officer whatever his name is who came over—"

"Drew."

"Right, Drew. He says, based on the description I gave him, it sounds like it, he, the man I saw in the house, resembles . . . your friend. Grey." The words are stilted and awkward and I want to slide under my barstool, but I manage to stay upright.

My drink arrives and I thank Jamison, taking the

time to get a sip of liquid courage down my throat. This is where she runs away screaming or tells me to get lost.

But she's not appalled or concerned for my sanity. Her eyes are wide and excited.

She grabs my arm. "What exactly did he look like? Wait—I have a picture." She fumbles in her purse and grabs her cell phone, tapping for a few seconds, and then turns it to face me.

Shock tightens my throat.

It's him. He's wearing hiking gear, boots, a back-pack, a dark blue baseball cap on his head. He's grinning at the camera and standing on a large rock outcropping, a sprawling valley and distant hills and mountains spreading out behind him.

There's no doubt about it.

The man in my house is the man in the photo. Grey.

Whatever she sees on my face has her grabbing my arm again. "Amelia, you have to help me."

Chapter Seven

"Help you with what, exactly?"

My mind is still tumbling. How could this man, this dead man, be the person I saw in my house?

Maybe he has a twin, a secret twin. An evil secret twin. One who likes to squat in other people's homes and can disappear at will.

Or maybe ghosts are not how Mom always explained it. I have to consider it, don't I? What other explanation is there for him appearing and disappearing in the same house he occupied when he died? I wasn't on drugs, and I've never hallucinated . . . What is going on?

"You did see him, didn't you?" Lexi stares at me, talking quickly. "You saw him." Her voice is full of awe. "You look like you just saw a ghost. Aren't you used to these things?"

I open my mouth to respond but she keeps talking.

"Did you talk to him? Did he tell you anything? Do

you think you can reach him again? Maybe we could do a séance." She bounces in her seat. "Can I come over?" The words are quick and excited.

I'm still in shock. She can read it on my face, I'm sure. Every drop of blood in my head has dropped to my toes. I need to pull it together. I'm supposed to be accustomed to ghosts, demons, and things that go bump in the night.

I blow out a breath. Is this why she asked me to hang out? Because she thinks, like my parents, I can communicate with the dead? I can't, and neither could they, but my mom was an expert at using her *real* abilities to convince people their loved ones were "communicating" with them. I didn't inherit even a fingernail's worth of her gifts. Instead of answering, I have my own question. "Are you sure he's dead?"

"Uh, yeah. I was at the funeral. But there are some things, um." She darts a quick look around the bar. No one is watching, but there are people at the bar close enough to overhear with little effort. "Let's go get a table."

We take our drinks over to an empty table in the corner. Lexi is jittering with barely suppressed eagerness as she slides into the seat across from me. Insecurity hardens like a stone in my belly. This is why she invited me out. My first real "friend" in town just needs a ghost hunter. What does it say about me that I don't get up and leave?

"After Grey died—" She stops and glances around

again before leaning closer. "His death just never sat well with me. Not that it would. He was my best friend, but I don't know." Her eyes drop and she bites her lip.

"You don't think it was an accident?" What do I make of all this? None of this was even alluded to when we talked about it the other day and she gave me the keys, or when she rescued me at the grocery store, but maybe she was just waiting for an opening.

"I don't know. There were the things that were happening in that cabin before he died, which is strange enough, but there's something else—which may or may not be related, but it made me suspicious." She hesitates. "You see, Mr. Blake also died, just a couple months before Grey did."

"Mr. Blake?" I've gotten two cards in the past twenty-four hours with that last name.

"Joseph Blake. He was Claire's husband—you met her the other day—and I understand Preston, their son, made an appearance at your place yesterday morning."

I tilt my head in acknowledgement. "He did."

She purses her lips. "Let me guess, he brought you a housewarming gift and it was something completely useless like an umbrella holder fashioned entirely out of rustic logs."

I laugh. "It was some kind of rare orchid, I think."

She huffs out a laugh. "Typical."

"Wait. How did you know he came by?"

She takes a sip of her martini.

"Wait, let me guess. Mrs. Jenkins at the bottom of my hill?

Lexi gives me a thumbs-up.

"Lovely. So were the two deaths connected or similar somehow?"

She shakes her head. "Not really. Mr. Blake had a stroke. He was older and had high blood pressure. It was unexpected but not out of left field."

"And Grey, how did he . . ."

She bites her lip. "He fell down the basement stairs."

I wince. Damn. Creepy basement again.

She finishes the last dregs of her drink in one smooth shot. "There's something else, in regard to Mr. Blake's death. Something I discovered recently that made me wonder."

"What is it?"

When she speaks, her voice is low, almost a whisper. "It's about Mr. Blake's will."

"Amelia. It's nice to see you again so soon." Preston stands at the end of our table, his eyes fixed on me, but they dart over for a split second. "Lexi." Her name is stiff and forced.

Before I can acknowledge his greeting, Lexi crosses her arms over her chest. "Preston. Fancy running into you here. Doesn't your type stick to the streets above Sixth?"

If there's an insult in there, Preston doesn't take the bait. "I was taking Mom home from her hair appointment and she wanted to stop in for garlic fries. You know how she is. I saw our newest resident over here and thought maybe I could buy you ladies a drink while we're waiting."

Lexi rolls her eyes. "We can buy our own drinks, P, but we appreciate your concern."

His jaw tenses. "I never said you couldn't, but Mother asked me to offer when she saw your cars out front, as it's the polite thing to do."

Lexi's eyes narrow but she lifts her chin.

Even an axe couldn't whack through the tension.

"Thank you, Preston. That's really nice of you to offer, for Mommy, but I think we're okay."

If Preston hears her, he doesn't let on, his eyes still on mine. "I heard there was an incident at your house last night."

My shoulders stiffen, my entire body tensing. Is nothing sacred in this town? "It was no big deal," I say quickly. "Just my imagination, I'm sure. Exhaustion. Long day of driving, moving is overwhelming, you know. But it's fine."

"If you ever have any problems with anything, you can always give me a call."

Lexi snorts.

"Is that funny?" His attention zags over to her.

She picks up her empty martini glass and clenches it in one hand. Will she use it as a projectile? My odds are on yes.

"What are you gonna do if she actually calls you and needs something? Send in your maid to fix it?"

His jawline clenches. "You shouldn't believe all the stories Grey told you."

"Whatever." She leans back in her seat. "Amelia is a grown woman. She doesn't need your help. Besides, she could probably whoop your ass while stabbing vampires and performing exorcisms."

I have to smother a laugh despite the hostility encircling this entire conversation.

His lips disappear into a thin line. "I have to go. Mother is waiting in the car. Amelia, it was a pleasure."

"Tell Claire I said hi," Lexi calls after his retreating form. Once he's out of earshot, she tsks. "I have no idea how Claire can be related to that tool. She's a class act but she spoiled his ass. Too much money and entitlement turns people into brainless dicks."

"What did he mean when he said don't believe the things Grey told you?"

She waves a hand. "Grey and Preston grew up together. Grey's mom, Bonnie, worked for the Blakes. Bonnie and Grey lived in a house on their property. She was basically a part-time nanny for Preston and she was also Claire's assistant. They were like brothers. And they fought like brothers."

"Oh." I still don't understand the strange animosity between Lexi and Preston. Yeah, he's kind of pretentious, but the total hostility? "So why do you hate him?" I ask, taking a sip of my drink.

"Grey was my best friend since we were in preschool. Preston is about three years older than us.

We all got along fine when we were young, but as we got older, Preston changed. And it wasn't the normal, older-kid-too-cool-for-the-younger-kids kind of thing. He was mean to Grey. Cruel, even. And Grey would laugh him off or make excuses for him." She shakes her head. "Grey was the best person. It's cliché, I know, but it's true. He was smart, funny, kind, silly." She smiles at some inner memory. "He was obsessed with the eighties, the music, the movies, the whole thing. If you said anything that even remotely reminded him of an eighties song, he'd belt it out just to make you laugh." Her gaze drops to the table, shoulders slumping.

Sympathy tugs at my chest. "I'm really sorry he's gone."

But sympathy is immediately followed up with self-doubt. Is Lexi grasping at anything that reminds her of Grey and using me to do it? Do I even care if she is?

"Me too." She sighs. "Anyway, he would mostly ignore Preston's behavior, but I can't. Not anymore."

"Why do you think Preston was mean to him?"

Her lips press together. "Jealousy."

"Jealousy over what?"

Her hand clenches around her glass. "I don't know. It made no sense since Preston had every advantage Grey did not, but I think it had something to do with Mr. Blake."

"Preston's dad? Claire's husband, the one who died before Grey did?" I clarify.

She nods. "Mr. Blake was like a father figure to Grey."

I nod, taking a sip of my drink and trying to absorb the intricacies of these relationships. "And you said something about his will?"

"After Mr. Blake died, there was a hold up in the processing of his estate. Not like probate, because he for sure had a trust set up, but I don't know why. He had his estate handled by a larger firm in Sacramento and not here locally. But right after Grey died, the trust was settled."

"How do you know this if the estate was handled by another firm?"

She smiles and leans her elbows on the table to get closer. "Most everyone knew there was a delay because Preston was getting pissy. He wanted to invest in some projects and couldn't because the money was tied up. As you've seen, you can't pee a different color without people in town finding out about it."

I laugh. "Obviously."

"Then about a year after Grey died, I met a clerk at a conference who worked in the law firm that handled the Blake estate. When it came up that I knew the family, she may have let it slip that there were some unusual documents in the trust. Documents that might be scandalous if they were made public and that's why Mr. Blake took his business outside of Mystic Falls."

"What were the documents?"

She shrugs. "I couldn't get more than that out of

her. Honestly, she shouldn't have even told me that much. But it seems likely that Mr. Blake left a portion of his money to Grey."

"And then when Grey died, it went to Preston."

"Exactly."

"And now you want my help because . . ."

"Because if you can, I don't know, communicate with Grey or something, maybe you can confirm if his death was really an accident or if he knows who killed him."

I chug down the rest of my drink and set the empty glass on the table. "I don't know. It doesn't really work that way. I'm not—my mom was the clairvoyant, not me."

That much, at least, is the truth. Yet with everything that's happened in the past few days, I'm almost willing to believe in the Easter Bunny, Bloody Mary, and Sam and Dean Winchester.

She reaches out a hand, covering mine briefly with hers. "It's fine. I totally get it. You can tell me no, you don't have to do anything. I thought it wouldn't hurt to ask. Honestly, it's just nice to have someone else to talk to about all this. I've sort of felt like a lunatic, you know? And no one else here could possibly understand."

Oh, trust me. I know. And she isn't upset, insistent, or rushing me out the door. Maybe she doesn't just want to use me for my "ghost" experience after all.

Aaaaand there goes the Tooth Fairy into the ladies' room.

"I'll do what I can. And if there's any other way I can help, just let me know."

Maybe if we solve this mystery, my ghost man will move on to the other side.

And why does distress strike me in the chest at that thought?

She smiles and then laughs. "You might regret that offer."

Chapter Eight

Snick.

Brightness flares against my closed eyelids.

I open my eyes, blinking rapidly against the light.

The light is on.

Why is the light on?

Squinting, I glare at the offending lamp. It's an antique gold monstrosity right next to the bed on the nightstand.

I know I did not fall asleep with that light on.

Bob is on the other side of the bed. She yawns and rolls over, exposing her belly.

No one is here. No hot intruder in a suit. Maybe it was some kind of power fluctuation or old, faulty wiring. I'll check it out in the morning. I reach over and click off the light, snuggling back into the covers.

Thump, thump.

My eyes open wide in the darkness but reveal nothing, still adjusting from staring into the light.

Is that a figure by the door? Staring at me?

My mind flashes with images of skeletons, bloody faces, and things from horror movies. I take a slow breath in and out.

The only haunting happening here are memories I can't shake. I squeeze my eyes shut, quelling the urge to hide under my pillow like a child.

The light clicks on again.

Taking a slow breath, I open my eyes to reach for the light again and—

A voice fills the room, thick and deep. "If you wanted to jump into bed with me so badly, you really should have asked first. I mean, it's the polite thing."

I leap up, grabbing the cup of water on my nightstand and chucking it at him.

"Jesus!" He leaps out of the way, but not fast enough. The glass hits him in the side and then thumps to the floor, water scattering all over the edge of the bed and sloshing onto the rug underneath.

Bob yowls and scampers out of the room.

"Bob, attack!"

She doesn't return. Figures. The one time I actually need her, she hides like a scaredy cat.

"Whoa, whoa, whoa." He backs up, climbs over the edge of the bed to get away from me, then stands on the opposite side, his hands up.

It's him. Grey.

Grey—who is dead.

I stare at him, my eyes so wide it almost hurts. He's breathing. He climbed over the bed. He's solid. What the heck?

He's speaking in low tones, something reassuring like, "It's okay, it's just me, everything's alright," but I barely register the actual words. "I'm not going to hurt you."

I pinch myself. Not dreaming. This isn't a dream. Then what the fuck?

"Did you just pinch yourself?" He smiles. Why isn't he freaking out? His hands are in the pockets of his dark sweats, his white T-shirt speckled with water.

"Maybe." The word comes out in a defensive clip. "So?"

His head tilts. "Are you a ghost?"

"What? No." How dare he accuse me of being the unalive person in this room. "You're the ghost."

"Am I?" His grin spreads and it makes me inexplicably annoyed. "You're the one who went all *Poltergeist* on me the last time I saw you."

My mouth pops open as I place a hand on my hip. "Well, it worked, didn't it? Freaked you out."

He nods, still smiling. "It really did. What's your name?"

I suppose it won't hurt to tell him. I cross my arms over my chest. "My name is Amelia. And I'm not a ghost. I was just pretending to be a ghost." I point at him. "*You* are the ghost."

My accusation doesn't bother him. Amusement still lights his eyes even as his lips purse. Then he shakes his head. "No. I don't think so." He glances down at himself. "I'm not decaying or pale or translucent so—"

"Neither am I."

Bob jumps up on the bed and prances over to Grey, sniffing him delicately.

"Hey, buddy." Grey reaches out to pet her.

I lift a hand, no doubt already too late to stop the mauling. "Don't—"

But I don't have to worry. Grey must have some ghosty voodoo that affects my cat because Bob isn't going into full-on attack mode. Instead of trying to kill him like she does to everyone else, she actually lets him pet her.

Then she purrs.

My mouth drops open.

This is more shocking than being in the same room with a ghost, watching said ghost pet my cat. And if he's petting her, then he's solid. Ghosts aren't solid.

"Are you an evil twin?" I ask.

"What?"

Bob moves away, then flops down on the bed and starts licking herself in the most inappropriate place possible.

Grey chuckles. "Well, that's awkward."

His eyes lift to mine and snares them for a heated second, the zing of recognition shooting through me.

I shake my head to clear it. "Okay. We need to figure

this out." I raise my voice and speak slowly. "How did you get here? Where did you come from?"

"I live here," he says, also louder and slower.

I huff out an exasperated breath. "You don't."

He's dead. I have to tell him. But standing in front of him, I once again question my own sanity. He's so real and solid. Lifelike. Not dead. He's just a few feet away, standing on the other side of the bed. In pajamas. It's surreal.

I shut my eyes and then press my fingers to my temples. Take a deep breath and exhale. "I have to be dreaming. It's just a really lucid dream. In three seconds, I'll wake up and you'll be gone again. You're not real. Not real."

The air moves around me. He's walking closer, his feet tapping on the hardwood as he approaches.

"Open your eyes." He's close. Standing right in front of me.

I shake my head. "No."

"Why not?"

Don't look.

I squeeze my eyes closed tighter. "You're not here. You're not real." I try the words again. Like repetition will make them true.

"Maybe *you're* the one who's not real and you're projecting your unrealness onto me."

Irritated, I open my eyes. "Unrealness isn't a word." He's less than a foot away. He has a teeny tiny dark freckle under his left eye. Why is that so cute?

Dammit, stop thinking about how hot the ghost is.

"You disappeared the other night." His voice is quiet and low, like he doesn't want to spook me. Can't blame him after the water incident and the whole, you know, acting like a lunatic stuff.

I shake my head. "No, *you* disappeared."

He laughs and I'm annoyed at how attractive the movement is. He has strong white teeth, sexy lips, a charming laugh, and he looks nothing like a ghost. It just doesn't make sense.

"This isn't funny."

"It's kind of funny." He regards me for a second, and then claps, making me jump. "Let's do an experiment. You game?"

My heart leaps. "I don't know. What kind of experiment?"

"Nothing indecent, I just want to touch you. Not to be a creep, just to confirm we're both real. No funny business, I promise." He puts a hand over his heart. "I'll just touch your arm or something."

"I'm not sure."

"Are you scared I'm right and you're the unreal one?"

"No." I bite out the word. "Fine."

I hold my breath, fists clenched at my side.

He touches my hands, his fingers tripping over my knuckles with utmost care. His fingers are warm, trailing up my arms and leaving goose bumps in their wake. Yep. I can feel him. I definitely feel something. I swallow as the heat from his fingers ignites an answering warmth low in my belly. How am I getting turned on by a touch on my arms? What is wrong with me?

"See? Real." His hands run up my arms, grasping my shoulders for a second, a brief squeeze, and then he pulls back and his hands drop to his sides.

I can't stop staring at his hands. He was just touching me. This is not a haunting. He is not a ghost. Then what is going on?

His brown eyes lock with mine. "How is this possible? How are you here?" I can't help it. I reach out, grabbing his middle and squeezing his sides.

He flinches and laughs, moving back a step. "Ticklish." He shrugs, his cheeks going a little pink.

Ghosts aren't ticklish. They can't blush. I have to tell him. "Grey, you've been dead for three years."

His smile falters, but instead of responding to news of his death, he asks, "How did you know my name?"

"I just had a conversation with Lexi about you yesterday."

His smile falters, but then his eyes narrow. "Lexi." Short laugh. He glances in the direction of the bedroom door. "Is this some kind of joke? She's nuts but I didn't think she had it in her to go this far. Last time was bad enough."

"No. It's not a joke." Are we doing this again? I knew I shouldn't have told him he was dead. I broke him.

He shakes his head. "You're a really good actress.

The creepy clicking noise the other night, that was classic. I hope she's paying you well." He heads for the door.

I stalk after him.

"Are you her new girlfriend?" he calls back to me, marching into the living room. "Fair warning, she's kind of a player. Breaking hearts all over the county, that one. If I had a quarter for every time I dried her ex-girlfriend's tears . . ."

"Lexi and I aren't a thing. We're just friends."

"Very funny," he calls, spinning around. "You can come out now." He stops, looks around and frowns. "Why are these back up?" He gestures to the Jesus picture and inordinate number of crosses. "I took them down when I moved in."

I stay silent. I've already told him the truth. What else can I say?

Regret slides through me, along with a touch of relief. If he sees what I do, maybe I'm not totally crazy. It doesn't explain how he's here and alive, but it's something.

He turns to me. "Where's my stuff? Did you hide my *Better Off Dead* poster and *Breakfast Club* Funko Pops?"

I shrug. I already told him he's dead. I can't explain anything else that's happening here.

His lips press together. "I'm not dead. I live here. Key word: live. I've been renting this place for a year. All my stuff was here an hour ago." He stalks back to the bedroom and I follow him.

He goes over to the closet and yanks the door open, wrenching on the cord to turn on the light.

Everything hanging in there is mine.

"No." The word is a surprised huff. He shoves the dresses to the side and steps into the closet.

As soon as he steps into the open space behind the hanging clothes, he vanishes.

Winks out of existence.

Gone.

Poof.

My stomach drops. "Grey?"

There's no response. No laughter, no arguing, no nothing. I push the clothes to one side, moving into the back space and letting the light fall over the wall. I run my hands over it, confirming it's intact.

And just when I think things can't get any weirder . . .

This is *impossible*.

Almost as impossible as having a dead guy show up in my house. Twice.

I press my palms into my eyes.

What kind of fucked-up Narnia shit is this?

Where is the logical explanation? There isn't one.

I knock on the walls—again—listening for the hollow sound of a space, but the wall is secure, no cracks, no indication of anything lying behind the closet. The office is on the other side, and there are no gaps between. I already checked all of that out.

I don't know what to do. I shut off the light and go back to my room, sitting on the edge of the bed.

Bob yowls at me from the doorway.

I toss her a glance and then check out the clock. It's two a.m.

I get back into bed. What else am I supposed to do? After a minute of staring at the ceiling, I turn the light off.

Then I lie there with my eyes open.

Maybe he'll come back. Maybe he won't. Maybe I'll never see him again. A bead of alarm bolts through my stomach. Why would I care? I don't even know him.

It can't be a hallucination or a dream. I felt him. I touched him. He was warm. He touched me. He smells like orange and spice and you don't smell hallucinations, right?

I need something. A plan. Something concrete and actionable. I can't control him showing up and disappearing. What can I control?

My mind's eye conjures an image of boxes of notebooks and sketches and books and drawings.

I do have somewhere to get guidance, even if it's a long shot. But is it?

My entire world has shattered and reformed again for the second time in my life, and my parents' journals are the only place that could have the answers. Despite the guilt pounding through me, filling me to the brim, and leaking out of my pores, I have to go through them.

It's the only way.

Chapter Nine

I used to love writing. It had always been a coping mechanism, a way to interpret things happening around me. It was self-therapy. It was how I dealt when I realized everything about my parents was a fraud, and it was how I tried to deal with the lingering guilt over their deaths.

But ever since their story went viral, it tainted everything. If I had a time machine, if I could go back and stop past-Amelia from hitting publish on that damn story, it would be my first stop.

I should sit down and write about my childhood, come up with some Hollywood-friendly story to satisfy Colleen.

But I don't. I need to figure out what's happening here and now before I go digging into the trove of information in my closet.

So, I write about Grey.

Bob sits behind my computer screen and periodically

stretches her paw around to bat at the words as they appear on the screen.

I write about that first night in the house, everything that happened, everything I saw, what was said, and how he disappeared. Twice. I write what Lexi told me about Grey, everything I can remember.

I sit back and consider the words, skimming over them and trying to get it to make some kind of sense. I don't know what to believe but putting it into words has the same cathartic effect that writing about my parents did, and it helps me step back and get a broader understanding of the situation at hand. And as I reflect over everything now, an idea niggles in the back of my mind. But it's impossible. Isn't it? Only one thing is very clear.

"He's dead, but he isn't a ghost. He can't be," I tell Bob.

"Who's dead but not a ghost?"

The deep baritone drives my heart into my throat. I spin around in the computer chair and gape. "You're back."

He's leaning against the doorjamb, arms crossed over his chest, biceps straining a white cotton T-shirt, strong forearms on distracting display.

"I guess I am." His eyes are wary, but he manages a small smile. "We have to stop running into each other like this."

"I think I know what's happening here."

His brows lift. "And what's that?"

I tap a finger on my knee and consider him. "What's today's date?"

His head tilts, but obliges. "It's Tuesday, October 6th."

"Okay, but what year?"

He uses his shoulder to push himself to standing, his gaze sharpening on mine. "2012," he says slowly.

I shake my head. "It's 2015."

"So . . . you're saying that you're, what, a time traveler?"

"I'm not. You are." I blow out a breath. "Maybe." Or he is a ghost, but ghosts aren't like anything ever imagined, and he clearly doesn't remember his own death. Maybe he's reliving the month he died in some kind of funky time loop? Maybe our time periods are somehow connecting? I have no idea. But we have to figure it out.

"Okay, *Quantum Leap*. Prove it."

I spin back around to my computer and open the browser window and then hesitate. I could probably find his obituary online, but maybe I should ease into the whole "by the way, you're dead" thing. Even though I already told him before, he clearly didn't believe me and maybe doesn't even remember. One traumatic experience at a time.

I pull up Google and type in "what's today's date" in the search box. When I hit enter, I lean back.

Grey rests a hand on the desk next to me, reading over my shoulder.

I give him a few seconds to absorb the words on

the screen. "It's not a trick and it's not a joke." I gesture to the screen. "Do you have any other explanation as to why all my stuff is here and yours keeps disappearing?"

He stares at the date on the computer. "No." The word is short, quiet, and loaded with disbelief. "How do I know you didn't set this all up somehow? Make a fake Google page or something?"

We lock eyes and then I gesture to the keyboard. "Go ahead and test it yourself. Do whatever you want."

He stares at me for a long second before hitting the back button on the browser and then typing "what is a bell that never rings yet it's knell makes the angels sing".

He hits enter, his arm brushing against my shoulder.

I squint at the screen. "What is Legend?" The answer to the riddle he typed is listed as a bluebell.

"It's from an 80's movie." He steps back from the desk, crossing his arms over his chest. "It seems like it's functioning normally." He uncrosses his arms, shifting on his feet. "This doesn't make sense. How is any of this possible?"

"What happens when you go back?" I match his low tone. He's so tense, I don't want to startle him.

His eyes meet mine. "Nothing." He clears his throat. "It's like I blink and everything is back to normal. To . . . my time, I guess." He blows out a breath and rubs the back of his neck. "Who are you anyway? You said your name is Amelia?"

"I'm Amelia Peters."

His dazed eyes focus and then narrow on me. "Peters. Paul's daughter? Gregory's granddaughter?"

"Yes. This was my grandfather's house. He passed away a few months ago."

His jaw tightens. "I just talked to him yesterday." He shakes his head. "I'm sorry, this is just incredibly . . . hard to believe."

A thought hits me. I want to ask him about my grandfather, but maybe now isn't the best time. Or maybe it's the perfect time since he might need a distraction from our current circumstances. "Did he, does he talk about me? My grandfather?"

He shrugs. "A little. And only after he found out your parents died. Sorry, about losing them. It was recent . . . Well, recent in my time, not so much in yours."

My shoulders slump, gaze dropping to my shoes. "Yeah. Thank you."

"He was worried about you after he found out about your dad. He prays for you."

I lift my eyes to his warm brown eyes.

I'm not sure how to process my grandfather praying for me. Happy that he cares? Or sad that he felt he needed to?

The conflicting thoughts must show on my face because Grey continues. "It's his way, you know. He prays for everyone he cares about, including me. I probably need it more than you."

I nod, and then we both stare at today's date on the computer screen in silence for a few long seconds.

"So . . .what do we do now?" he asks. "Why is this happening? Is there a way to stop it or control it?"

"I'm not sure exactly, but I do have an idea on how we can find out."

I get up and walk over to the closet, sliding the door open.

I turn to pick up the nearest box, then face Grey and lift it in his direction. "Here."

His brows lift as he takes the box from my hands. "What's this?"

I take a deep breath. "It's research." I swallow. I can't believe I'm doing this. I've been avoiding these books since they died, and now not only am I going to read them, I'm going to hand them over to a veritable stranger to dissect and judge and think the worst of me and my family.

What are our other options? Google? Not if we really want to find out what's happening here. Mom would know. She knew things, impossible things, all the time. When I was seven, we stayed with a family for a few weeks after the father had passed. Mom was talking to his widow in the kitchen, and in the middle of the conversation, she stood, walked over to the window, and asked Dad to take down the curtains. He did, and lo and behold, the deceased had rolled up cash and hidden it inside the curtain rod. Mom helped the widow locate thousands of dollars her husband had hidden throughout the house.

If I could talk to Mom . . .

I shake my head.

She's not here. Ghosts don't linger. They move on. They leave behind impressions, sometimes, and she would pick up on it—but actually communicating with them? Never.

These journals are the closest thing I have to speaking with her directly.

Some instinct pokes at me, telling me that Grey won't judge, that I might actually feel better about reading these words with him, and not just because he's experiencing something just as mystical as what we're going to read in these journals. There is something about Grey's presence that is soothing and familiar. I'm safe with him, my gut tells me, and Mom always said to trust my gut.

I grab another small box from the closet. "These are my parents' journals." I turn back around just in time to catch Grey's eyes flipping up to my face.

Was he checking out my ass?

Am I sort of excited and flattered that he was checking out my ass?

Pull it together, Amelia.

"We may be able to find something we can use to figure out what is going on. Maybe it's something that happens only when you're . . . when you're . . ." Flustered, my bravado sputters out. I can't just blurt out that he's dead. Again.

One corner of his mouth tips up. "Uncontrollably handsome? Charming and mysterious?"

I smile. "Yeah, sure. Let's go with that. It might be a long shot, but my parents wrote about a lot of strange things."

"Oh, right. They were like, voodoo witch doctors."

"Paranormal investigators."

He nods. "I would definitely classify this as an experience outside the norm."

I clear my throat. "Anyway, we can go through them to see if there's anything comparable. Maybe some kind of, I don't know, solution? Explanation?"

He looks down at the box in his hands. "A vague plan is always better than no plan."

Without protest he follows me into the living room. I set the box on the coffee table and open it up, passing Grey a book when he sets the other box next to mine.

"And what am I searching for in here, exactly?" As he sits on the couch, Bob hops up next to him and settles at his side.

"Anything that might explain why we're living in two different times and somehow able to see each other, I guess."

"And touch each other."

My face heats. Was that suggestive? "Right."

I sit on the opposite end of the couch and open a small, red, leatherbound diary.

Grey shifts next to me, opening the book in his lap. Bob purrs at his side and he absently scratches her head before flipping the page.

I watch him for a few seconds and then stare blindly down at the pages in front of me.

Is it weird that this isn't weird? Like this guy—who's dead, who I barely know—is sitting here reading my parents' journals with me, searching for things about, I don't know, time travel, like this is an everyday occurrence or something.

Smoothing back the cover to the first page, I swallow and then read, blinking at the handwriting on the page as familiar as my own. My heart lurches in my chest.

Oh, Mom.

I miss her. I trace a finger over the lettering and then try to concentrate on the actual words.

Kansas. 1999.

Memories flood me as I read Mom's perspective of that night.

They did some hocus-pocus ceremony under a full moon for Y2K to avoid the bad juju and find prosperity in a new century and all that. They charged, of course.

Everyone drank mead, and Mom gave palm readings while Dad did tarot cards.

Mom gave me a reading that night. The memories rush back with her words.

Amelia has a twist in her fate line.

I wish I could warn her, but the fates are intricate beasts and one false move could alter the path.

Warn me about what?

I told her what I could, and I just hope she remembers. There is no such thing as a coincidence. Coincidence is the universe showing you your path. There are always signs and you must heed them.

I shake my head. Typical Mom. Ambiguous and impossible to interpret.

Grey shifts in the seat next to me. "I'm hungry. Do you want something to drink or eat or whatever?"

Jerking with surprise I meet his eyes and then glance into the kitchen. "Oh. Um . . ."

"Oh, wait." He winces. "Sorry. It's your kitchen. I probably shouldn't be offering your own food to you." His brows lift. "You have anything good to snack on? I missed second breakfast." He rubs his flat stomach and I try not to stare.

"Yeah. I just went grocery shopping."

"Perfect. I'll get snacks for both of us."

I start to stand and he stops me with an outstretched hand. "I got this. As long as you don't mind me raiding the fridge and cupboards?"

"Fine by me." I settle back down in the seat and keep reading.

The next story in the journal is from Dad.

They shared their journals, and so the handwriting flips back and forth from her small script to his bulkier, scribbled penmanship.

His entry is about a woman whose spouse died. They helped her commune with him, ultimately discovering that he'd been living a double life and had been murdered by a secret girlfriend.

This is the kind of thing I should be writing for

Colleen. She would love this. Murder, ghosts, sex, mayhem. But it's not what I want to write about. It's all bullshit anyway. I mean, except the murder part. That was probably legit.

Cupboards open and close in the kitchen while Grey whistles something, *Walk Like an Egyptian* maybe? Well, whatever it is, it's nice having someone here, the comforting background sounds of companionship. I've almost forgotten what it's like to not be eternally alone.

I skim through half the notebook and then glance in the box. How many are there? These two boxes have at least twenty journals each. There are four more boxes in the closet, but not all of them are full of journals. There are a few with stones, jewelry, and other books on herbs and spells and who knows what else.

"Here." He sets the food on the coffee table.

I blink at it. He's covered the cutting board in an assortment of snacks. Crackers are spread in an artfully arranged S, surrounded by salami, grapes, chunky cheese portions, blueberries, nuts . . . It's like something from a Pinterest board, one of those pins that I save because it looks amazing, but I never actually attempt it. "Wow. Thanks."

"No worries." He pops a cracker and cheese in his mouth and takes his place back on the couch next to me.

I grab a few grapes and try to focus on the book in front of me.

The next page is an article that's been pasted onto the page about how the atoms and elements that make up the human body are the same elements that make up the stars in our galaxy.

We are stardust, Mom wrote underneath it.

I shake my head, smiling.

These journals are full of witchery mixed with facts and science—because the best way to con someone is to mix the truth with the lies. It makes the lies even more believable, after all. It's how conspiracy theories gain so much ground.

I scan pages, moving through the journals faster—periodically stopping to reach forward and grab an apple slice with cheese—but nothing can explain Grey. No mentions of ghosts who are solid, people coming back from the dead, people from another time. Nothing.

"These journals are really interesting."

"You think so?"

"They traveled a lot." He reaches over to the coffee table to grab more food. "You were just a kid and you moved with them?" He shoves a thick pile of crackers, meat, and cheese into his mouth in one bite and chomps.

He's demolished about half the tray and I've barely touched one corner. "Yeah."

"That must have been hard."

I rub my thumb against the sharp corner of the journal. "It was normal for me." It only got hard when the truth came out. Or what I thought was the truth.

He looks up and meets my eyes. "That makes sense. It's hard for me to imagine since I've only lived here and in Eugene."

"Eugene?"

His gaze dips back to the book in front of him. "It's where I went to college. What was the best place you went?"

I consider the question. "I would have to say . . . Blythe."

"Blythe? Where is that?"

"Southern California. It's only about 200 miles outside of LA, hotter than hell, and kind of a small town."

"Why was it the best place then?"

I shrug. "Maybe it wasn't the *best* place, but it was my favorite."

"Why?"

I glance over at him. He watches me, curious.

I don't want to tell him the truth, as it's sort of embarrassing. But something makes me speak honestly anyway, maybe because he seems like he actually cares. "Because I had a friend there."

He flips a page. "You didn't have friends in other places?"

I shake my head. "It's probably lame—"

"Absolutely not lame," he interjects.

"But I didn't want to leave. I was twelve and there was this girl, Sarah. She was just," I shrug, "really accepting and nice. We went for walks, watched movies, built forts and did silly things together. It was a connection. I'd never had that before with someone my own age." My cheeks heat. "I could tell her anything, you know?"

"How long did you live there?"

"Two months. And that was one of our longer stays in one place."

He shakes his head. "How did you ever manage to get through school when you moved around like that?"

"I was mostly homeschooled. Then I got my GED when I was sixteen."

"Wow. I can't even imagine."

"What about you? What was it like to grow up in the same place your whole life?"

"Good," he says but then stops and considers. "And bad, sometimes. Everyone knows your business or wants to know your business—especially in a town this size. Dating is almost impossible because the options are limited and you've known most of the people your whole life so it might be like dating your sister."

"But you had stability and you always knew what to expect."

He nods slowly. "That's true. I guess there's a good side and bad side in every situation. Or, as they say, every rose has its thorn."

I laugh. "Ain't that the truth."

"Bret Michaels speaks no lies," he says solemnly.

We read for a few more minutes, but curiosity about him keeps nibbling at me. "So . . . college in Oregon?"

"Yeah. But I didn't finish. I only lived there for two years."

"What happened?"

He averts his eyes, dropping his gaze to the book in front of him. "My mom died. So, I came home."

"I'm sorry."

He shrugs. "It's fine."

"I know what it's like," I blurt out. "To lose your family. To not have . . . anyone."

Our eyes lock and it happens again, that sense of recognition, an awareness that flows between us.

"What was he like?" I blurt.

His brows dip. "What was who like?"

"My grandfather."

He nods and considers me for a second before responding. "He's cool. I mean, I like him. He's a good landlord. He doesn't talk much. He's very serious, very devout. He doesn't have many close friends that I'm aware of, but the pastor knows him really well, up at St. Matthews."

I nod. Pastors and church people don't really like me once they realize who I am, who my parents were. Heathens. Satanists. Occultists. Bad guys.

The estrangement makes more sense, then. Dad always says he was into the paranormal from a young age and clearly his father was a devout churchgoer with a bajillion crucifixes. Those two things wouldn't rub along together well. It explains a lot. But why didn't Dad ever talk about it? Was it that bad?

We continue to read and eat, stopping only to talk about things we find or to use the restroom. The sun descends, casting lengthening shadows on the floor.

We make it through three of the boxes, and once it's full dark outside, my eyes are crossing and I need a major break.

I flip a page, blowing out a long breath. "I don't think I can take this anymore. Maybe we should do something—" My breath catches in my throat.

A scribbled phrase leaps out at me in Mom's precise script.

Time slip.

"What is it?" Grey asks.

I drag my eyes from the page and meet his curious gaze for a second before looking back at the words on the page.

Underneath *time slip* is a smattering of other phrases.

Temporal distortions, a wrinkle in time, a crack in time, tesseract, worm hole, portals, Bermuda Triangle. Outlander.

"Outlander?" I roll my eyes.

"Outlander?" Grey asks.

"Look at this." I scoot toward him and he meets me in the middle of the couch, reading over my shoulder.

"Time slip?" His breath puffs against my cheek.

I flip the page. A news article is pasted onto the next sheet from some scientific journal in Australia. "'Scientists send particles back in time,'" I read.

Underneath it, I trace a finger under more notes from Mom.

Within the realm of Einstein's general relativity, a

person could travel through a wormhole and go back in time.

"This has to be it. Time travel," Grey says, excited.

I skim the words on the page. The article is mostly Greek to me, but the gist of it is that time travel itself is merely a portal through space created by energy fluctuations in positive and negative directions. These fluctuations each create a curved space that opposes the other. If these two were then connected, you would have a wormhole. If it lasted long enough, theoretically a particle could be transported through.

I flip through the next few pages where more articles have been pasted onto the pages, stories from around the world, news reports of people moving through cracks in time.

In between each article, there are more handwritten notes from Mom. One where she describes talking to a woman in Bakersfield who got on the freeway and a second later ended up on a military base fifty miles away. *Worm hole*, she wrote next to that one. *Government experiments*. There are other reports from New Mexico, Nevada, Ohio, all about people missing chunks of time and blaming aliens, but under some of those are Mom's interpretations. *Someone changed their past.*

I flip another page, and Dad's scrawling script takes over.

"Check this out." I read the words out loud. "'When I was eight, I saw my first ghost. Or what I thought was a ghost. But it wasn't a ghost. It was a real, live person.'"

Chapter Ten

I stare at the words. Is this it? Is this what we've been searching for?

"Holy shit," Grey mutters. He leans closer, the heat of his shoulder pressing into mine, his eyes skimming down the page.

"Eight." I point at the number. "Dad was eight when this happened. Which means he would have been living here, in this house. Grandpa bought the house from the Blakes when Dad was just a baby, according to Claire." My heart beats faster. I try to focus even though my thoughts are scattering.

As if he can sense my distraction, he holds out a hand. "Can I read it out loud?"

I nod and pass him the book, our fingers brushing.

He reads, his voice a soothing low bass. "She was a teenager, dressed in a long white dress, strange and frilly. It covered her from her wrists to her ankles. Her name was Constance Smith. She appeared in my room nearly every day for a week. At first, I would hide and pray. I thought she was a ghost or a demon. But then one night I retrieved a toy from my parents' closet and ended up back in her time—the house was the same but changed."

He stops. "Well, this sounds about right."

He clears his throat and keeps reading. "'The furniture was different. There were no appliances. No power. No running water. Constance was there. She was kind. We talked.'" Grey huffs out a laugh. "Your dad wasn't one for long, eloquent speeches."

I chuckle. "Nope. He was always a concise communicator. Mom was more of a talker, but they were both good at being vague." Because that's how you got people to believe your lies.

But . . . were they lies?

Grey continues. "'I tried to tell my father, in my naivete thinking he would help me. Instead, I got the switch for it. No more blasphemy would be allowed under his roof.

"'It was the first time in my life I didn't heed my parents. Constance and I were convinced this was happening for a reason. I went to the library and searched through old newspaper microfilms to find out as much as I could about her life, and I soon discovered why we were connecting. I found an article about her death.'"

We share a glance.

He turns the page and then sucks in a quick breath

of surprise. "I've seen this before." His finger runs over the page. It's a photocopy, worn with age and some of the ink has faded, but it's mostly legible.

"Really?" The headline reads *Murder in Mystic Falls.*

"Joe showed it to me once when I was, I don't know, I guess I was a teenager maybe. This lady, Constance, was his great grandmother. Wow. And your dad saw her. The whole thing with their great grandma is sort of a family legend."

Joe? Oh, he means Mr. Blake. I raise my brows, waiting for him to continue.

"He didn't tell me she was a time traveler or anything, just that her dad tried to kill her." He frowns and his gaze returns to the murder headline. "But she didn't die. She survived."

"Not according to this article."

"Wait." He flips through to the next page. "It was this one." He stops and points at another news story. "This is the article Joseph Blake had in his study."

Attempted Murder in Mystic Falls, the new headline reads. It's the same font and formatting as the prior with one big difference.

"Huh. One word really changes the outcome."

He flips back and forth between the two articles, trying to take it all in, and then back again to the first one.

We both read the contents in silence. The article describes how Constance was found beaten, bludgeoned to death, and the main suspect was a farm hand who was traveling through the area.

Dad's writing continues underneath and Grey reads it out loud. "'I went through the slip to tell her what would happen to her. Maybe it wasn't supposed to happen that way. Maybe we could change her fate.'"

He flips the page to the second article. The date is the same as the first, and again we read in shared silence. In this one, Dad describes how Jedediah Smith—Constance's father—attempted to kill her and she managed to elude him.

Grey reads the words scribbled underneath the second article. "'Constance was anticipating the attack and was able to defend herself and flee.'"

"Holy shit," I breathe.

Grey looks over at me. "Your dad changed the past."

I meet his eyes and then stare down at the newspaper article. It's all laid out in black and white. Is it possible? I suppose the first article could be some kind of forgery, but . . . what would be the point? Besides, it explains what's happening right now.

"What does this mean?" Grey asks, pointing out the next passage. "'Constance and I took a spell in the in between. Not sure how time passes there. When every-thing turned back to colors, she was gone.'"

"The in between?" I frown. "What is that?"

"I'm not sure. 'When everything turned back to colors,'" he repeats the line. "Wait. I think I know what he's talking about."

"You do?"

"I think I've been there." His eyes lock with mine. "It's like a dream place. And he's right. It's a weird, colorless place."

The dream. The sexy dream. Suddenly heated, I lean away from him under the pretense of taking a sip of my water. Was that real? The dream where I was in bed and . . . was that Grey? It did seem like everything was sepia toned and not quite reality. *The place without colors.* No. No way. There is no way in hell I'm going to ask if he had the same sex dream. But that sense from it, knowing that the person behind me, touching me, was someone important, someone who knew me intimately . . . Not just physically intimate, but everything in between. What if it was Grey? What if that's why I'm so comfortable with him, like I've known him my whole life instead of a day?

Flustered, I gulp down more water and then return the cup to the side table. "Yeah, I'm not sure what he's talking about. Let's keep reading."

Grey's lips tug up, and the glance he tosses me is amused, but he keeps reading. "'Things had changed. My own existence and life in Mystic Falls was not the same as before. At first, I didn't remember Constance. It was like it had never happened. But in my gut, I knew something was off.

"'It wasn't until I found the original article pressed between the pages of a book that the original memories returned. The photocopy of the original article had survived the change in history. Maybe because it was in the secret compartment in the closet, where the portal seemed to be the strongest.

"'She never appeared again and I couldn't go through the slip anymore. The portal had closed, its purpose served. The time slip exists for a reason and once that reason is fulfilled, it's gone and all memories of those involved are altered.

""Constance went on to marry Adam Blake and they had Thomas Blake, who had two sons, Joseph and Don. Their family became a part of Mystic Falls history, its members now influential and wealthy.

"'In the old timeline, the one where Constance died, Adam went on to marry Doris Flanagan, and they were unable to bear children. The Blake line ended with him.'"

Grey rubs his chin. "The Blakes. This is such a trip. If your dad hadn't saved Constance, Joe wouldn't have been alive. Preston wouldn't be alive."

I shake my head. It's a lot to wrap my head around. "I can't believe it."

"But this isn't the first time you've dealt with paranormal stuff, right?" He gestures to the books spread out on the coffee table, detailing my upbringing in all its abnormal glory.

I look up at Grey. We're still sitting close enough that our shoulders touch, his face only a few inches from mine. I could tell him the truth. Who's he gonna tell anyway? And it's strange, and I wouldn't believe it if

I weren't feeling it for myself, but I know I can trust him.

I take a deep breath. "It kind of is."

"Care to expound upon that comment considering we are knee-deep in your parents' journals full of ghosts and goblins and other somewhat supernatural mysteries?"

"I've never told anyone."

His eyes widen. "Now I'm intrigued."

"You can't tell anyone."

He nudges me with his elbow. "Who am I going to tell? Oh, hey, I know this big secret about Amelia Peters because I travelled through a time portal to when she's living in my house three years from now and forcing me to read her parents' diaries."

I laugh, but the humor fades when I consider my next words. "My parents were con artists."

His lips purse. His eyes flick over to me and then down at himself and then back at me again. "Really?"

I nudge him with my elbow. "Okay, so maybe they weren't total liars. My mom knew things, and she could read people sometimes, but the hauntings and places we went where people would pay for them to get rid of ghosts? There were no ghosts. They lied. They made things up. They made people believe and then 'got rid of it' so they would get paid. It wasn't real. It was never real." My voice quavers in the middle, but maybe he won't notice.

"Everyone knows those paranormal things are fake. I

mean, c'mon, it only takes watching one episode of *Ghostfacers* to see it's a bunch of dudes running around in the dark with a shaky cam, jumping at every noise and saying, 'Did you see that!?' over and over again." He flips to the next page. "Although now I'm questioning my own thoughts and theories on all that." He splays a hand between us. "Obviously."

I blink down at the words in front of me. Is he right? Am I overthinking everything I know? Maybe my "big secret" isn't as bad as I thought. Maybe I shouldn't have judged my parents so harshly, but I already know that.

A warm palm covers my jean-clad knee. "Hey. It's okay. Do you want me to keep reading?"

I nod.

His hand moves away. "'Maybe some hauntings are actually past happenings that need to be fixed. Just like ghosts sometimes linger when they are taken too soon—when what has come to pass was wrong and not actually meant to be because even the fates make mistakes, but then the universe presents the opportunity to correct them.'"

"So, the portal opened again because of you." The words pop out before I can think about them too much.

"Because of me?" He frowns but then his expression clears. "That's right. You said I died."

I don't know what to say.

"You said I've been dead for three years. The other night in your bedroom. And then earlier, you said, 'he's dead but he isn't a ghost.'" He swallows and then blows out a breath. "I think it's pretty clear, based on all this," he gestures to the books around us, "you need to tell me everything about my death." His eyes meet mine, penetrating and intense.

I hesitate. I have to tell him everything I know. But how? How awful to be told the details of your own death.

And before I can muster the nerve to say anything at all, he disappears.

Chapter Eleven

The journal he'd been holding between us flops to the couch, the cover slapping against my thigh before tilting over onto the couch.

I blink at the empty seat next to me, the air still lingering with his scent, the heat from his arm against mine slowly cooling.

"Grey?" I roll my eyes at myself. Why am I calling for him as if that will somehow conjure him back into existence? He clearly doesn't have any control over it.

I pick up the journal and skim over the next few pages, but it goes on to another story. Another haunting. No more time slips or anything helpful.

I shut the notebook and chuck it onto the other side of the couch.

Bob immediately pounces on the discarded book and gnaws on the corner.

Why did the universe take him at the worst moment?

We need to talk about this and what it all means. Clearly the universe opened the portal because of Grey's death but . . . I didn't even get a chance to tell him when he dies or what happens.

My head slumps back against the couch.

If Dad's theories are true—and let's face it, I have nothing else to go on—there's a reason the time slip is here. What if Lexi is right and Grey was murdered? That has to be the case. Right? Because if it truly was an accident, just telling him what happens should prevent his death. He could just avoid the basement on Halloween. But if it's not an accident . . . we're supposed to stop it somehow.

But how?

What would happen if I did save him? If he never died? It would change the future, I mean, the present, right? And everything in between. Would I even be here now? Would Grandpa have let him continue renting and not left the house to me in his will? Then I never would have met Grey to begin with.

My head hurts. I lie down, curling up on the couch, putting my head on the side where Grey was sitting.

What if it's already too late? I don't even know how time passes there. What if it's faster than here and when a couple days pass here, it's been weeks there? No. That can't be right since it's the same day in his time, and just the years have changed. What if he never comes back?

The thought makes my heart lurch in my chest.

I blink open my eyes and stare at the fireplace and bookshelves.

What the—?

I'm in the living room. I sit up and glance around. I fell asleep on the couch. Bob rubs her head against my leg and then jumps up next to me.

"Grey?" I call out.

Nothing answers me but silence and Bob's purring.

Grey. He left before I could tell him . . .

I get up and put on the kettle. It's only seven in the morning and my back is killing me. Reminder to self: do not fall asleep on the couch. While the water heats, I jump in the shower to let the heat soften my stiff muscles, my mind just starting to wake up and mull over the events of the past week.

One very important thought pounds through my brain: I need to prepare him like Constance was prepared. Which means I need to know exactly when, where, and how he died. As much info as I can get. So far, I only know he fell down the basement stairs. Or maybe he was pushed.

After I shower and change, I grab my laptop and head to the living room, half expecting Grey to reappear, but the house remains silent and empty except for me and Bob.

A quick google search brings me face to face with Grey's obituary.

A black and white head shot sits in the corner of the page.

Gone but not forgotten, the heading reads.

I skim through the short paragraph.

Greyson Michael Holmes passed away at his residence in Mystic Falls, California, on October 31st, 2012. He was twenty-three years old.

So young. Two years younger than I am now.

Grey was a star student and athlete at the University of Oregon at Eugene. He was an NCAA swim championship medalist two years in a row and was on the dean's list multiple terms. He has left behind many friends. He was preceded in death by his mother, Bonnie Holmes. Services will be held at St. Matthews. November 30th, 2012.

I blow out a breath, staring at the words. I can't believe it's real, not when he was just here sitting with me, reading with me, eating with me . . . touching me.

I shiver.

Now I know the date he died, but maybe Lexi knows the time, too. I pick up my phone to call her, but it's seven in the morning. Perhaps too early to call someone and discuss details of their best friend's demise.

I'll call her later. Now, I just have to pass through this time portal and tell him. Should be simple, right? I mean Grey doesn't even know it's happening when he crosses over into this time.

If Dad could do it and Grey can do it, I should be able to go back, too. I head for the bedroom, heart pounding in my chest. I'm seriously going to try to time travel.

I come to a halt in front of the closet.

Dad said this is where he first went over. I'll start here. Makes sense with all the closet weirdness that happened when I first moved in.

I yank on the light, shoving my clothes to one side and then sit cross legged on the floor. I shut my eyes and . . . think about time. Hmmm. Clocks. Past. 2012. *Outlander. Bill and Ted's Excellent Adventure. Outlander.* Mmm, men in kilts. After a few silent minutes, I'm still sitting here and nothing has changed.

Bob prances in, crawls into my lap, and purrs, her rumbling filling the space.

This is ridiculous.

Pushing to my feet, knocking a disgruntled Bob off my lap, I move toward the rear of the closet. This is where he disappeared right in front of me the other night.

I lean my forehead against the wall. Nothing. I tap around, but I've done this before and it didn't work then so I'm not sure what I think it will do now.

I turn around and slump back against the wall.

Bob sits at my feet, stares up at me, and meows.

"I know. I want to see him, too."

Let's not analyze that statement too much. I am not attracted to a ghost man. Okay, maybe I'm a little attracted to a ghost man, but nothing can ever come from it. He's dead. My job is to help him, not lust after his sexy forearms and charismatic smile.

My phone buzzes in my pocket, and I jump, banging my head against the closet rod with a yelp.

Who is calling me at eight o'clock in the morning?

"Hello?"

"Hey, it's Lexi."

"Hey." I rub my head. That's gonna bruise.

"I have some news and I wanted to talk before I go into work. Are you home?"

"Um, yeah." This is useful. I can get the timing of Grey's death while she's here.

She pounds on the front door, the sound penetrating both the phone and the walls of the house. "Come let me in."

I exit the closet, shutting the light off on my way out and making my way to the front door. "You're here?"

"I know, it's early. I'm sorry. But I come bearing donuts."

"You're forgiven. I was awake," I say as I open the door.

"You always up this early?" She breezes past me, a whirlwind of perfume in a pressed and polished pink pantsuit, and heads straight to the kitchen.

I follow her. "Most of the time." Especially when I'm anticipating an erstwhile dead guy from the past to pop in at any moment. Wait. What if he shows up while Lexi is here? That would not be good. It might be traumatizing for a dead ex-best friend to appear out of thin air.

"Have you had any other incidents?" she asks.

"No." The word pops out a hair too quickly. "Oh, but I did want to ask you something about Grey's death."

"What is it?"

"Do you know what time he died?"

She pops open the box of donuts, raising an eyebrow at me. "They place the time of death between eight p.m. and midnight on October thirty-first. Why?"

"Um, it will help me commune with him. Maybe." I nod. I'm terrible at this. "So, what did you need to talk about?"

She hands me a donut along with a flimsy napkin. "I have other news about Grey."

"Do you want some tea?"

"Sure."

I open the cabinet and pull out mugs and tea bags, setting them next to the donuts.

Bob jumps up on the counter a few feet away and stares at Lexi.

Lexi gives her the side-eye. "Is she going to snap?"

I shrug. "Probably not. She mostly reserves her attacks for men." Except for Grey, for some reason.

"Smart cat. Anyway, remember how I told you I went on a date with that clerk who knew about Joe Blake's will?" She shoves a chocolate crème donut in her mouth and chews.

"Sure."

She finishes chewing before she speaks again. "I took her out again last night."

"And?" I open a tea bag and dunk it into my mug.

"And I may have plied her with martinis and then convinced her to give me more details on the Blake Family Trust."

I stop making my tea and stare at Lexi. "What did she say? Anything helpful?"

She nods. "Sort of. Instead of just mentioning there are strange documents in the will, she told me what one of them is, specifically."

"What is it?" She takes another bite of her donut chewing carefully and I roll my eyes. "Now you're just being dramatic for effect."

She laughs. "It's a paternity test."

"A paternity test?" I muse. "What do you think that means?"

"I think it means Grey might have been Mr. Blake's actual biological son."

I lean sideways against the counter. "Holy shit."

"Yep."

"So wait, who does Grey think his dad is?" It didn't say in the obituary, it just mentioned his mom.

"He doesn't know who his dad is. His mom never told him. Bonnie was an amazing woman, but she was tight lipped about it. It was the only point of contention between them."

"Wow." Why wouldn't she tell him? Did she not know? Maybe she didn't tell him because Mr. Blake was his dad . . . and Preston is older than him. Claire and Joe must have been married when Grey was conceived. What a mess.

So now, not only do I get to tell him how he died, I also get to break the news about his possible paternity.

"But we don't know for sure if he's the baby daddy," I say.

"We could know for sure," she widens her eyes at me, all innocence, "if we had some DNA samples."

"DNA samples? From who?"

Joe is dead. And so is Grey. Well, sort of.

"Preston."

I take a sip of coffee and connect the dots. "Oh. Yeah. That makes sense. If they are brothers, that would prove Joe is his dad."

"Exactly. I have a friend who can expedite some DNA processing, and I have boxes of Grey's old stuff, which includes a hairbrush with plenty of his DNA."

"So that takes care of Grey's DNA, but how exactly are we going to get Preston's?"

"I have a list of things they can use."

She pulls a piece of paper out of her purse and hands it to me.

Cigarette butts, floss, toothbrush, hair, blood, sperm, fingernails, ear wax, mucus.

Gross.

"Does he smoke?"

"No."

"Might be weird if I offer to clip his nails or clean his ears."

She taps her chin with one manicured finger. "Hair might be the easiest to get."

"Okay, but how? Are you going to break into his house to steal a hair brush?"

"We don't need to do anything illegal. But to be on the safe side, we need a well-thought-out plan." She gives me a cat-like grin that's scarier than Bob's death glare.

"I have a feeling I'm not going to like this."

She laughs and throws a tea bag at me. "Don't worry. This will be fun."

Chapter Twelve

"I can't believe you talked me into this."

"Relax. It's going to be easy. Just get some of his hair, then run away if you need to." She peeks around the corner of the building, scanning the parking lot for Preston.

"Oh, yeah. So easy. What was it you recommended again? Tell him he has a bug in his hair and then just reach over and yank out some strands?"

She laughs. "I thought you would appreciate that one more than my other suggestion. But I wouldn't ask my worst enemy to sleep with Captain Pee Stain."

We're hiding around the side of the Mystic Falls Country Club, which is nestled in the middle of a sprawling golf course. The country club itself is an enormous brick and rock McMansion with tennis courts on either side and an Olympic-sized pool in the rear.

Lexi convinced me to call Preston and ask him for

help with something—men love feeling superior, she said—and he suggested we meet for brunch here.

Lexi came with me, mostly for moral support and also so I can pass off the sample once I've retrieved it—however I manage it—and take it to a lab to be cross-referenced with Grey's DNA.

Lexi rambles about how sexist the golf club administration is because they won't let her be a member, and she's thinking about suing them, but I have a hard time focusing on the conversation.

I had another one of those dreams last night. At least, I think I did. This one wasn't sexy, though. I can't remember much except the vibe of it, the general weight-lessness and lack of color. Grey might have been there, but I'm not sure—I woke up and was dismayed he was still gone. I'm still tired, like I never quite woke up.

Lexi, still peering around the corner, jerks back. "He's here."

"Should I go in?"

She stops me with a hand on my arm. "No, give him a minute to get a table."

I can't believe she convinced me to go through with this. What if it doesn't work? "I don't think I can just yank his hair out."

She puts her hands on my shoulders. "Amelia. Not only can you do this, you absolutely should behave as odd as possible. You want him to think you're a freak, because then he'll leave you alone. This is like two for one. Get his DNA and get him to go away all at the same time." She nods. "Trust me, you don't want him to like you. You can do better. Crazy Lou, that old lady who crashes the city council meetings and rants about aliens stealing her body parts? She can do better than Preston, too."

I sigh, shoulders slumping.

"That's the spirit." She releases me and jerks her thumb in the direction of the entrance. "Now go get that double helix."

"Fine."

"Text me if you need an emergency rescue. I'll be waiting right here."

I take a deep breath and make my way to the front entrance of the McMansion.

It's been two days since I last saw Grey. He's probably fine. I mean, he's not fine. He's still dead. But I'm sure he'll show up again before it's too late. He has to, right? Hasn't the universe already decreed he has to survive or whatever? Isn't that why I can see him in the first place?

Why doesn't that make me feel better?

The interior of the building is all vaulted ceilings and skylights, exposed beams giving the space a rustic, yet luxurious ambiance when laid out with the tiled floors and creamy walls.

A grey-suited woman with a sensible bob stands at a desk in the front, a wide staircase leading up to the second floor behind her. Men in colorful pants and women in white skirts and polo shirts amble about, their murmuring voices echoing in the open space. It smells like money and snobbery.

The woman in the suit points me in the direction of the restaurant, and when I find it, the maître d' points me in the direction of Preston's table. Everything is white and shiny—white table cloths, white flower center-pieces, white walls, white clothes on the people present—except for the pants. Even though Preston himself is wearing those funky golf pants and a polo shirt, every-thing is so pristine. I'm underdressed in my black slacks and plain white button-up blouse with kitten heels.

When I approach, Preston smiles and stands, pulling out my chair.

"Amelia, it's lovely to see you again." He leans forward, one hand on my shoulder, his lips moving toward my face.

What is this? Is he going to kiss me?

There's an awkward shuffling where I try to turn and make it into a hug, but his face is still veering toward mine and oh dear, he's going in for a cheek kiss, like we're in Europe or something. His lips land somewhere on my hair while I try to give him a side squeeze.

If this moment could be framed, it would be called, *oh no.*

I laugh, the sound smothered with nerves.

We manage to sit down across from each other without any further incidents. I meet his eyes and then the worries start to multiply.

I'm too far away to reach any of his hairs.

Dammit, I should have grabbed some while he was trying to kiss me. Maybe I'll have to wait until we're leaving, get him to walk me out. Then at least I can be close enough to him to rip out some hairs.

What if we just sit here and stare at each other in misery for an hour?

"I took the liberty of ordering some blintzes, eggs benedict, and quiche."

"That's great, thanks." And a little domineering. What if I was lactose intolerant? Or a vegan?

"I also ordered a tea service." He gestures as the waiter brings us a tray loaded with gleaming tea cups and a matching tea pot, the elegant handle honed with silvery vines.

My eyes widen. "Oh, this is wonderful. I love tea." Maybe this won't be so bad, after all.

They even have little delicate sugar cubes and fancy tweezers.

He takes a minute to pour and hand me my little tea cup. "So, what was it you needed my assistance with?"

I take a sip and relax against the plush seat.

Here it is. Moment of truth. On the phone I was intentionally vague, and now I have no idea what to say.

But maybe there's a way I can actually make this brunch worth my while.

"A couple of things actually." I fiddle with the fork closest to me. "Since I moved into town, some people have been . . . a little unkind."

He winces. "I'd heard some rumblings about that."

"I know you grew up here, so I thought you might have some suggestions on how I can, I don't know, fit in? Get people to know that I'm not a bad person. You've been so kind." I mean, he has, despite what Lexi likes to say about him. He's been a little odd and overbearing, but not unkind. Not to me, anyway.

He nods. "My family has lived here for so many generations, so just being seen with me should help the rumors." Okay, so also a little egocentric, but whatever.

"Any other tips?"

"I would recommend volunteering. You should talk to Mother about it. She volunteers at the hospital and at almost every town festival, and she contributes to a variety of local causes."

"Great. Those are great ideas, thank you."

He nods.

And then conversation stalls. I take another slow sip of tea, but I need to do something else. Ask something. Figure out how to get his hair. I eyeball it, hoping some strands will just magically fall out, or I can wish some out through sheer force of will, but it doesn't seem to be working.

"Have you had any other problems up at the cabin?" He takes a sip of his tea, one pinky in the air.

I'm about to open my mouth to tell him no. But then I change my mind. If he is the murderer, maybe I can get him to talk about Grey. I can determine if he appears homicidal while discussing their relationship.

"It's funny that you've asked, because I actually have

had some encounters," I drop my voice, "with the afterlife."

His brows lift, but before he can ask me to clarify, our food arrives.

The blitzes are delicate and perfect, arranged in a circle with orange and berry garnishes. The quiche are minis filled with a variety of meats and veggies and fruits. The eggs benedict is smothered in creamy hollandaise. The waitress assembles everything on the table between us.

"These are egg whites only, right? That's what I ordered." Preston gestures to the quiche.

She nods. "Yes, sir."

"It better be," he mutters.

Does he realize the eggs benedict is mostly yolks? And now I understand some of Lexi's animosity. Yanking out his hair is becoming a more enjoyable prospect.

He dismisses the waitress with a clipped, "That will be all."

"Thank you," I tell her, smiling extra wide to try and make up for Preston's behavior. I guess Lexi isn't totally off base about him.

Without waiting, I load up my plate with some of the food. It smells heavenly, egg whites or yolks, none of it matters to me.

"So." Preston picks up one of the servings spoons and carefully places a single blintz on his plate. "What were you saying about the afterlife?" he asks before picking up his fork to eat.

Grey keeps magically appearing and then disappearing because of some weird time portal thing, oh and hey, can I have some of your hair?

"A mysterious shadowy figure that comes and goes." I take a bite of quiche but keep my eyes on Preston for his reaction.

He nods down at his plate and a crease appears between his brows. Is that concern for me or disapproval of the way the powdered sugar was dispersed on the blintz?

"There was a voice, too."

He looks up. "What did it say?"

I consider my words carefully. I need to be vague, and yet give away enough to give him pause. "He asked for help."

Preston flinches. It's a small movement, over in a blink. "He?"

I nod and force out my next words. The lies aren't easy. They don't roll off my tongue like they did for my parents. Once I knew the truth, I would cringe and shudder on the inside no matter how skilled they were at convincing others. But Preston being a dick to the waitstaff gives me enough chutzpah to proceed. "Spirits often linger when they have unfinished business." I focus on the blintz on my plate, cutting off a bite with my fork before lifting my gaze back to his. "I know you were close with the prior resident, and I was wondering if you knew anything about his death or why his soul would choose to linger."

His lips thin and he reaches for his tea. "His death was an accident. Grey and I grew up together, but we weren't close when he died."

"Do you remember anything in the month he died? Was he acting strange or did he mention anything to you about . . . anything?" Best to leave it sort of open ended.

He frowns down into his cup. "No. Nothing. I don't think we even spoke in the months leading up to his death, other than at my father's funeral. But listen, you probably shouldn't talk to other people about this."

"Why not?"

"Because if you want people in this town to like you, this won't help. They're already suspicious you're going to use the death of a local to further your career."

My hand tightens around my fork. I don't want to write anything. And I have to wonder, is that actually the case, or does he not want me asking questions because he's guilty?

Although, if he had actually done it, wouldn't he instead say things about how they were childhood friends or whatever to avoid suspicion? Aren't murderers sneakier than this? Unless he realizes Lexi would contradict any bullshit.

Before I can figure out how to respond, an elderly gentleman stops next to our table. He's tan and grinning, dressed in a white polo shirt, white shorts, and spotless white sneakers. His arm is wrapped around a much younger brunette wearing a similar outfit but a skirt instead of shorts. Her hair is shiny and long and she's holding a tennis racket in one arm. Must be his daughter or something.

"Preston." He puts a hand on Preston's shoulder.

"Uncle Don." Preston nods in greeting and then gestures to me. "This is Amelia Peters."

"Ah, yes, Gregory's granddaughter. I heard you moved into the Peters cabin." His eyes are appraising, his smile widening.

I nod and smile. Hm. I didn't know Don had a daughter. No one mentioned her.

The brunette clears her throat and presses her shiny lips together in what might be a frown.

After a silence that goes on a fraction too long, Don says, "Oh, this is Patsy."

"Betsy."

"Hi Betsy, it's nice to meet you." I stick out my hand.

She smiles shyly and takes my hand, holding it a little too long and rubbing her finger on my wrist. "It's nice to meet you, too. Maybe we can join you for brunch." She lifts wide eyes to Don.

I pull my hand away, tucking it in my lap.

He grimaces. "Not today, sweetie. She's not my type."

Betsy frowns, pushing out her lower lip.

"We'll slum it some other time." He waves a dismissive hand.

I blink. What? Is he talking about me? Was Betsy wanting . . .?

Slum it? My mouth is hanging open and I close it with a snap. Part of me is disgusted, and the other part of me wants to tell him that I am amazing in bed and kinkier than I look, and a threesome with me would never be *slumming it.*

Preston sighs. "Don, Amelia is my guest today."

Don just laughs and then pats his date on the arm. "Behave, okay, sweetie?"

Is he reverting to "sweetie" because he can't keep his girlfriend's name straight? This guy is gross.

Also, did Preston just stand up for me? Sort of?

"It was nice to meet you, Amelia. Preston, I'll see you this weekend."

They leave and Preston turns to me. "Sorry about that. Uncle Don is . . . well, he's too old to change."

I'm not sure I can take much more of this. "It's not your fault. But, uh, can I get a box to go?"

Chapter Thirteen

"So, thank you for brunch. It was really nice."

This is it. I have to do this, and I have to do it now.

Maybe I shouldn't have taken the to-go box of food, because now I have one less free hand, but oh well.

"It was my pleasure. Can I walk you to your car?"

Oh crap. Here's a level of chivalry I wasn't expecting. Time to kill that bird with a big stone.

"No, that's fine, it's—" I open my mouth and shriek like the hounds of hell are racing toward us.

Startled, Preston glances around, probably worried about who might be watching instead of bothering to ask me what's wrong.

I'm too embarrassed to even peek around. I might end up eighty-sixed from this facility, but I don't really care. I have no choice. I'm not going out with him again, so I have to get this done.

I point at him and then flap my hand next to his head, my leftover box slamming against his shoulder.

He dodges my maniacal fingers. "What are you doing?"

"It's a bee! Hold on, don't move." I shout, overly loud in the pristine setting.

Is he really buying this?

My performance must be convincing enough because he freezes, his eyes going wide.

I slap him on the side of his head and then immediately pinch and yank as much as I can from the same spot—maybe he won't notice, what with my box also flapping around his head.

"Ow!" He flinches away, but it doesn't matter.

"I got it. I think."

He backs away from me, rubbing his head.

I fiddle with my box, hiding the hand clutching the dark strands behind it.

"It's gone. You're welcome."

He blinks at me, mouth hanging open like he's not entirely sure what just happened.

I can't blame him. I'm not sure what I just did either. My face is so hot, my hair might burst into flames.

"Thanks for brunch, uh . . . I'll see you around."

I don't want to lose or expose the strands I'm clutching, so instead of waving, I do a clumsy head nod and then hustle around the side of the building, out of sight, where Lexi is still waiting.

She's doubled over, laughing so hard she can't speak.

"I'm so glad to amuse you." I attempt to be wry, but her hysterical laughter forces a chuckle past my lips.

"I can't believe you smacked him on the head." She clutches at my shoulder, nearly falling over and taking me with her.

Then we're both cackling like a couple of lunatics.

Once we've managed to control ourselves, I hold up my hand. "You better take this before I drop it."

"That was the best thing I've ever seen. I haven't laughed so hard since . . .ever." She stands up straight, wiping the mirth from her eyes and then rummaging in her purse.

I hold out my hand with Preston's hair. "If that doesn't scare him away, nothing will."

She snorts and takes the hair, sealing the baggie and tucking it away. "You might be surprised."

I gape at her, humor gone. "You said this would get him to leave me alone."

She shrugs. "Never underestimate the self-absorbed. They'll put up with a lot for even the slightest hint of an ego boost. But don't worry, I've got your back." She grins at me and then links her elbow with mine, tugging me toward where her car is parked behind the building. "Thank you for helping me. Thank you for being my friend."

The words wrap themselves around me like a warm cloak in the middle of a snowstorm. I have a friend.

Lexi blows out a rough breath. "It's been difficult since Grey died and I've been . . . well, it's been lonely, you know? But now, for the first time I feel like I have a person." She tightens her arm on mine.

I swallow past an unexpected lump in my throat. "Of course. I know what you mean. I haven't had many close friends, ever." Heat flushes up my neck at the admission, but Lexi just squeezes my elbow tighter.

She smiles, cheek dimpling. "Well, now you do. And just so you know, this goes both ways. If you ever want me to go out with someone and bash them in the head for you, I'm all yours. Even if it's a man." She grimaces. "I'd still take care of it for you."

I laugh. "That's quite the sacrifice. I'll keep it in mind."

The cursor winks, taunting me in the middle of the blank page. I need to write something. Something I can actually share with Colleen. But I can't.

I don't want to do this, so why am I doing it? Because it's expected? Because I don't want to let people down the way I let my parents down? When does it end?

I spoke with Colleen again this morning. "This is your future, Amelia," she told me.

But it isn't the future I want. I don't want any part of this. I want something different. I love writing, but not like this, not at the expense of my parents. Myself. Everything.

This isn't supposed to be my path. The thought

sinks into me, fusing into my very bones. This is all wrong. This was never supposed to happen this way.

Just like Grey isn't supposed to die. That's not supposed to happen either.

I think.

It's been four days now and he hasn't reappeared.

I've continued to read through my parents' journals alone, but it's slow going and so far, I haven't found anything useful. I've tried going into the past myself, but that continues to be a bust. I guess I'm just not cut out for time travel.

Honk, honk, hoooonk.

I move toward the window. Distantly, people whoop and holler, but I can't make out the words.

Why would anyone be honking and yelling in my driveway?

I pull back the curtain and peek outside. There's a car driving away, a small dark sedan of some sort, spitting up gravel as it zooms down the drive and disappears.

My eyes lift to the tree in front and I curse.

One of the biggest trees has been accosted, toilet paper hanging in long white strips, fluttering in the breeze.

It's like, three o'clock in the afternoon. Really? They don't even wait to TP me until it gets dark? Clearly, they don't care if they're caught.

"Bob, people suck. Be thankful you're a cat."

Once the dust settles from the retreating vehicle, I

head outside and attempt to pull the toilet paper from the branches of the large pine.

One tug and the fragile paper breaks off in the middle, most of it still hanging on branches far above my head. How the heck did they get it up there so high? I guess it's easier to toss it up than it is to yank it down.

I need a ladder.

The shed. I haven't done much more than glance inside, but I think there was a ladder in there.

It takes me a minute, but I manage to get the wooden ladder opened and set up against the tree, convincing myself all the while that I can do this. I'm a homeowner and a bad ass. I don't need help.

Just don't look down.

I move up the ladder a few steps and tug at the flimsy material, but it's not enough. I'll need to get higher.

Wait. What's this? A white square of notebook paper flutters in the breeze, impaled to the tree with a nail.

Let the dead rest, witch!

"Would that I could," I mutter. I crumple it up and drop it to the ground to be thrown away later.

I continue to tug on the toilet paper, getting down as much as I can without endangering my very existence. If I fell and broke my head open, how long would it take the authorities to find me? I suppose Lexi would come searching eventually.

Maybe I should call the cops and report this.

No. No way. That's all I need, more reasons for the

people in this town to hate me. I'll just clean it up as much as I can and call it good.

I guess calling me a witch is preferable to being called a bitch. Right? Maybe?

Wait. *Witch*.

Mom had a witch's spell book of some sort she found in an antique store. Maybe there's a spell or incantation or something in it that will help me get my time traveling groove on so I can go back to Grey's time. There are also stones and herbs and other things in some of the boxes. Maybe that would help . . . open the portal or whatever.

Once the idea catches, I can't shake it. It's something to do. Purpose flows through me, lightening the stress of worrying about Grey and wondering what the hell I'm doing with my life.

Moving faster now, I finish cleaning up most of the mess, although I end up leaving some of the paper high up in the branches, and then hustle back inside.

I grab the box with the stones and witchy things and proceed to put on every piece of jewelry I can find that will allegedly enhance any mystical abilities.

I locate the spell book and open it to the table of contents, skimming.

A spell for finding lost things. Hm. Well, I'm not really lost, but I would like to find Grey, so maybe that sort of applies.

There are also some spells for manifesting your

wants and desires . . . I don't want to think too closely about how accurate that is in regard to Grey.

I bring everything into the closet, yanking on the light and sitting in the center and reading the words out loud.

"Be it high in the air or low on the ground, let what I'm looking for now be found."

I repeat it a few times and then blow out a breath. I feel like an idiot.

I flip though some of the book, hunting for other spells that might apply.

"I don't seek. I attract. What belongs to me will simply find me."

Wait. Was that a thump? My ears strain, trying to pick up anything through the silence.

"Jesus!" I startle as Bob prances into the closet and curls up next to me.

Great. I've manifested my cat.

I stand up and try walking in and out of the closet multiple times while chanting the spells.

Nothing.

I grab an old white candle from the box, but I can't find any matches or a lighter, so I end up with the flashlight, sitting in the middle of the closet with the lights off, and chanting more spells.

Still nothing.

Shutting my eyes, I think about Grey. His dark, sleepy eyes, his expressive mouth, his laugh, the way he smiles and that freckle by his eye. Nope. Then I try thinking about Jamie Fraser.

All this is doing is making me horny.

This is ridiculous and it's not working, but I can't give up.

An hour later, I'm sitting in the closet, legs criss-crossed, covered in jewelry and rocks with a tinfoil hat on my head and my eyes shut, still trying to manifest a time portal.

What if I never see him again? The thought is oddly depressing.

"What are you doing?"

My heart leaps as my eyes fly open. He's here.

Chapter Fourteen

I gape up at him. He's naked. Well, not entirely naked, more's the pity. His hair is wet, the dark strands dripping onto the collar of my robe. He should look ridiculous, but he doesn't. He's entirely too comfortable in his own skin and that doesn't change, no matter what he's wearing. Even if it's a pink and purple robe with a cat head hood.

For a minute, I'm completely discombobulated. Did he somehow go through the slip while he was in the shower? He's just washing his hair and accidently time travels? How is it so easy for him?

He crosses his arms and leans against the doorjamb, a smile tugging at his lips. "You're cute when you look like a homeless gypsy hiding from the government and preparing for an alien invasion."

A rush of mortified heat blows through me.

I wrench off the tin foil hat and fling it on the floor at my side. "Well, Mr. Smug, it worked."

"What worked?"

"I was trying to get back to your time, but instead I helped you come forward."

Maybe. Possibly. I mean, probably not.

I push myself to my feet and flick a hand at him. "Since you're here again. Finally."

"I am here." He points at himself. "Nice robe, by the way."

I flush. "It was a gift."

"I'm not judging, I'm appreciating."

The robe is shorter on him than it is on me, exposing strong calves, tan forearms and a sliver of his collarbone.

Appreciating? Yeah. Me too.

I stomp on those thoughts and attempt to focus on more than naked Grey in my robe.

His smile drops and he rubs the back of his head. "So, not to ruin all the fun, but last time I was here, I sort of went back before you could tell me about . . .well, you know."

I fidget with the hem of my shirt. Dammit, there's a dirt smudge right up the middle of my pale-yellow shirt. Maybe I should have changed after playing around up in the tree.

"Yeah, that's why I've been . . ." I gesture to the gems and jewelry all over me, the tin foil hat and spell book on the floor. "I've been worried you wouldn't cross back over before . . . before . . . "

"D-day?"

His wry tone startles a laugh out of me. "Seriously?"

He shrugs. "I've had some time to come to terms with it. We need to talk more about the details—before I disappear again. The more info I have about how this happens, the better I can prepare."

"Right. And there's been some other developments. Let's go to the kitchen. I think I left my computer in there."

He nods and then follows, a palpable presence behind me.

He's back. He's not dead. Relief swells through me. It's like something has clicked into place, some missing puzzle piece. And having him here, not being alone, is a singular type of joy, even if I have to have a conversation with him about his own death and possible paternity.

My laptop sits on the dining room table. I set it on the kitchen counter where we can both read the screen.

Maybe I should try to ease him into the whole "this is your obituary" thing and also Mr. Blake is potentially your father stuff. I face him. "I can pull up your obituary? Is that okay?"

He blows out a breath. "This is still so unbelievable." He crosses his arms over his chest and then nods. "Go for it."

I wake up the screen and then pull up the webpage I read the other night.

He stops me with a warm hand on my arm. "Wait.

Before I read that, can you just tell me how it happens and when?"

His eyes are troubled, brows low, the corners of his mouth creased down. This must be so strange and unbelievable for him. I can't imagine someone telling me about my own death. He must be terrified. "October 31st. It was an accident. You fell down the stairs in the basement. It happened sometime between eight p.m. and midnight. At least, that's what they think."

His brows shoot up to his hairline. "I fell? On Halloween? That's my glorious end? Tripping and falling down some stairs?"

So perhaps he's not exactly *terrified*. "What, you think it should have been in some kind of epic battle? This is Mystic Falls, not Waterloo."

"Was it at least a dark and rainy night?" He waves a hand. "Fine, fine. Never mind. Let's see it."

I already know what it says, so I keep my eyes on Grey as he scans the screen.

A few silent minutes pass, long enough for him to read it through three times.

"Are you okay?"

"As okay as I can be reading about my own death. It's a little surreal. October 31st is only about three weeks from now." A dent appears between his brows. "What if I just leave town or something? What then?"

I shrug. "For all we know, that would just push the date back and not actually change anything. You're here, in this time, learning about this for a reason."

He nods.

"Lexi thinks your death was suspicious. And I think, considering everything, she might be right, but also there's something else."

I explain what Lexi told me about Mr. Blake's will and how there was a delay. "She doesn't know exactly what the documents said, but she found out one of the attachments in the trust was a paternity test."

He stares at me and then blows out a breath, leaning against the kitchen counter. "A paternity test? Wait. She thinks Joe was my father?"

"I went to brunch with Preston the other day because she needed his DNA sample to test. We don't know anything yet for sure." I wait, letting him mull all of this over. "Lexi is supposed to be calling me when she has the results. She did everything she could to expedite it, so hopefully soon."

One hand lifts, rubbing the back of his neck. His eyes fall shut. "It might actually explain a lot of things."

"Like what?"

He swallows and then meets my eyes. "Like how my mom would never tell me who my father was."

He looks away, out the windows spanning the rear of the house, gaze unfocused.

We stand there in silence and I'm not sure if I should leave him for a minute to his thoughts or what, but then my stomach growls so loudly, he lets out a startled laugh. "Hungry?"

I wince. "I guess I missed lunch. Are you hungry?"

"I can always eat."

"I have frozen pizza." I head toward the fridge.

"Perfect. And if we have to have this conversation while I'm half naked, it might require a drink."

My cheeks heat at the reminder that he's naked under my robe. I cool them off by sticking my head in the freezer.

"You wouldn't happen to have any clothes that might fit me?"

I peek around the door at him. "No. Sorry." Absolutely not sorry. Biggest lie I've ever told.

Once the pizza is in the oven, I pull a bottle from the cupboard. "Red wine okay?"

"That's great." He opens one of the cupboards and gets the wine glasses down, then sets them on the counter. "So, you said you went to brunch with Preston to get his DNA? What does that mean, exactly?"

"I had to get a hair sample." I pour wine into both of our glasses.

"How did you manage that?"

"Let's just say it was unlike anything I've ever done, and that's really saying something."

He stares at me for a beat and then cracks a laugh. "Knowing Lexi, I bet it was interesting. Did you tell him anything about what's going on?"

I shake my head. "No, of course not. If he killed you because you're his brother and he didn't want to share his immense inheritance, we can't let him know we know. We haven't confirmed anything yet, but that's in process. Lexi has someone who can test his DNA."

"Wait, how is she going to test his DNA with mine? If I'm dead, doesn't she need something from me?"

I take a sip of my wine and then move around him and into the living room. "She has all your old personal belongings, which apparently includes one of your hair-brushes."

He tsks, following behind me. "Figures she would keep those things. I always knew she was obsessed with me."

I sit on the couch. "She does care about you a lot."

He smiles, rueful, taking the seat next to me. "She is my best friend. It's weird to think about being dead and all my earthly belongings having to go to someone. She would be my choice—I have no living family, so she's the closest thing to it."

I nod and then frown. Where would my belongings go? I only have Bob.

"What do we do next?" He takes a sip of the wine.

We. I like being a we. "What do you mean?"

He sets his glass down on the end table next to him and turns toward me. "What if he is my brother? Then what?"

"Then I guess it could be a motive."

His lips purse. "I'm still not sure he would have it in him to kill me. He's not the most trustworthy or humble, but murderous?" He frowns. "And is money a reasonable motive? Their businesses do well and I can't imagine him wanting to kill me over it. But even if he did, how would you prove it?"

"Maybe we can't. But maybe if you know it's him, you can be prepared the day you're supposed to . . ."

"Kick the bucket? Meet my maker? Get un-alived?"

I sigh. "Yes. All those things."

The oven timer dings and I stand up, but Grey is already on the move. "I've got it."

He cuts the pizza and brings our plates back to the living room.

We eat our food and sip the wine in silence for a few minutes before Grey speaks again. "All of this, it really makes me wonder about my mom's death."

"Why?"

He doesn't meet my eyes, gazing into the corner, expression distant. "Didn't Lexi tell you? Her death was ruled a suicide."

I suck in a breath. "No. Oh, I'm so sorry."

He looks at me. "That's the thing, though. I never believed it. We had made plans that weekend. I drove down from Oregon. When I got home, I found her slumped over the kitchen table, an empty pill bottle next to her." He sets his plate to the side. "There was no note, but there was also no sign of forced entry, no defensive wounds, nothing to indicate she wasn't alone."

I reach out and put my hand on his arm.

He covers it with his other hand and then glances down at our hands. "You're cold. I can start a fire."

"Do you want me to do it?"

"No, it's fine, I need to move." He gets up to push the button and keeps talking. "Everyone told me I was wrong. They said it was just the grief. They said there was no other explanation. No possible way her death was anything but a suicide. But I still can't believe it. And maybe it is just the grief talking, but I knew my mother better than anyone did. After graduation, we were going on a trip to Alaska. One of those old people cruises. She had wanted to do that forever. Plus, that weekend, she told me she had something important to tell me. People with plans don't kill themselves, do they?"

I sit back on the couch and pick up my wine glass. "I don't know. I don't have any answers. What do you think she wanted to talk to you about?"

He shrugs and takes a drink out of his glass. "I don't know. I had been bugging her for years to give me more information about my dad. When I was young, I didn't really think about it, but when I was in high school, I started asking more questions. We were close. It was the one thing she would never tell me. She'd clam up. She wouldn't tell me anything about him, not his name, not if he was alive somewhere, not if he was dead, nothing. The most I got out of her one night was when we were arguing. I yelled at her for keeping information from me and she told me she was ashamed."

"Ashamed of what?"

He shakes his head. "She never said. She told me she was ashamed, and she cried and I never asked again. I couldn't stand seeing her unhappy. She was never unhappy. She was like . . . sunshine. She made cookies. She never swore. She never yelled. She was basically Snow White. Birds would follow her, and animals would dress her in the morning. I was so lucky to have her, and I should never have pushed her for something she couldn't give me."

"Maybe she didn't want to tell you because your father was a married man."

His face pales, the flickering light from the fire revealing his stricken. A crease appears between his brows. "He would have been married when I was . . . conceived." His eyes drop with a wince.

We sit in silence, thinking, stewing, sipping our wine.

Bob jumps up into Grey's lap and settles, like she knows he needs the comfort. I stare at her. Why is she so different with him than with every other man ever?

"How long ago did your mom pass?" I ask.

He pets Bob's head and she shuts her eyes and purrs.

Can't say I really blame her.

"Three years. For me, anyway. Six in your time, I guess."

"And Mr. Blake died just a couple of months before you."

His head tilts in question. "And?"

"I guess I'm just wondering if your instincts about your mom are correct. Maybe it wasn't suicide. Maybe it's connected somehow to your death. If someone had enough to lose or gain by getting you out of the way, why not her, too?"

He considers my words and then shakes his head. "I want to believe it, but there was no evidence of foul play. No break-in to our house. Everyone says people who commit suicide never act like they're going to."

"They ruled your death an accident because you didn't have any evidence of forced entry either. And clearly, we don't believe it was an accident. What if it's someone you know? You would feel comfortable letting them in, you know? If you were both murdered, you must have known them. Like, if it was Preston, would she have let him in her house?"

"Yeah, probably. But what would he have to gain from her death?"

"If she was about to tell you that Mr. Blake is your dad, apparently a lot."

He shifts forward on the couch. "I don't know. You want some more wine?" He stands up and reaches for me to hand him my glass. "I'll get it. I need to do something."

"Do you want to read through more of the journals? There could be more helpful things in there." I twist to face him.

He pours more wine in our glasses. The tension in his shoulders relaxes a notch at the suggestion, the crease between his brow shrinking. He nods. "That would be great. I need a distraction, a purpose. I don't know, something else to focus on."

"Well then. Let's get busy."

Chapter Fifteen

"I might have to steal this. It's amazingly comfortable." He rubs his hand on the fabric covering his shoulder, then lifts up the neckline and sniffs it.

"Are you sniffing my robe?"

We're in the living room, reading, fire still blazing. The windows are black panels of darkness, but inside it's all cozy and warm, like we are in our own little world. I've changed into my comfy lounge pants and T-shirt.

"You smell nice. You know what else," he sniffs it again and then frowns, "you kinda smell familiar."

We've moved closer together. Every time one of us gets up to grab a book or refill the wine or get some water or a snack, we end up nearly touching in the center of the sofa.

"That's not creepy or anything." I flush with embarrassment—and because everything about him is familiar to me, too.

"It's not creepy." He sniffs again. "It's more . . . unusual."

"Is that a better adjective?"

"What's wrong with unusual? I'd say it's better than creepy. I'd rather be odd than normal, actually."

"Well, you've accomplished that goal."

"I'd say we have that in common, tinfoil hat lady."

I laugh. "You can't steal it. It's one of the few things that bring me joy." Maybe I shouldn't admit that. I duck my head, staring down at the page in front of me.

He reaches over, his hand warm as it covers mine just for a split second. "I need joy, too. I'm the one who's dead. Besides, I wear it better." He leans even closer, our shoulders brushing together. "Maybe I'll disappear with it on and then request to be buried in it. Then you'll really never get it back."

I shake my head. "You know, you're surprisingly flippant about your own death."

"I think I'm in the denial stage of grief." He pauses. "Can you grieve your own death?"

"I don't know, is inappropriate humor one of the stages?"

He laughs, eyes alight with humor and appreciation. "Obviously."

I grin. It's sort of thrilling, making him laugh.

His gaze dips to my mouth and then back up so quickly, I might've thought I imagined it if it weren't for the instantaneous rush of heat it pumped through me. "Besides, I've got these newfound time-traveling abilities because I'm supposed to live forever." He taps on the page with his pointer finger. "It's a total trip that they changed history. Isn't there a thing about that? Like it's bad? Butterfly effect and whatnot? Like even changing one minor thing can cause a total space-time continuum disaster?"

"In movies maybe. But this isn't *Back to the Future*."

"Except that's literally the best eighties movie."

"No, it's not."

"Uh, yeah it is."

"*Labyrinth* is the best eighties movie."

He considers this. "Not a terrible choice. Okay, fine. Maybe time is more like the multiverse."

"What do you mean?"

"You know, like in the Marvel comics. There are multiple realities, multiple branches of time with different existences. There's another Amelia out there somewhere with three kids and a husband living in Iowa."

"Iowa? Really?"

"That's the part that throws you off? So, you could be married with kids in another reality?"

"Not likely. I can barely get past a third date in this reality." Did I just admit that out loud?

"I find that hard to believe." His dark gaze sharpens on mine.

"You shouldn't."

"Why do you say that?"

I gesture to the journals spread out everywhere. "You

know how much I moved growing up. That continued through my teen years, so there was no opportunity for the whole first date thing, no prom, no . . . none of it." I wave a hand like it doesn't matter, but it did matter.

When I was seventeen, I left. I went to LA and worked in restaurants and tried to figure out what my life was without my parents, without the paranormal, without being a part of something I hadn't believed in for years. But establishing connections was so hard. Everyone was already a part of a group. They had people they'd grown up with, friends from high school, elementary, coworkers, connections that were established. I tried to fit in. Most people were nice enough but I always felt like I was an interloper, just on the outside. Present, but not quite fitting in.

"What about after high school?"

"I dated here and there but nothing serious. What about you?" I nudge him with my shoulder. "Any girlfriends I should know about? Especially since a scorned ex-lover could be a prime suspect."

His grin is slow. "If you want to know if I'm single, you could just ask. I am, by the way. I know, I know, restrain yourself."

"I'll work on that," I say drily. "So, no ex-lover. Anyone else want to kill you that you know of?"

"Of course not. Who would want me dead? I'm adorable."

"Apparently, maybe, Preston doesn't think you're so adorable?"

He chuckles. "Maybe. Preston and I haven't been close in a long time, but at Joe's funeral, he brought me over to sit with the family and asked me to be a pall-bearer with him and Don and some of Joe's friends. He was genuinely distraught and still thought to include me."

"That's nice, but it doesn't mean he's not a killer."

He puts the journal aside and turns to face me. "But we can't focus so much on one person we miss someone else. Does Lexi have any other ideas or is she stuck on Preston?"

"She hasn't mentioned anyone else to me."

"Yeah. She's never been a fan. But if the only motive is money, he's not the only one who might benefit by getting me out of the way."

I nod. "There's Claire."

He barks out a laugh. "Claire? Claire can't even kill spiders. She rescues stray cats and volunteers to hold babies at the hospital—she's basically an angel. She and my mother were good friends and she was like a second mother to me. She helped raise me, more or less."

I shrug. "Maybe they seemed like they were friends, but if Joe is your dad and Claire found out—"

He's already shaking his head before I've even finished my sentence. "If I die on Halloween, she'll have an alibi. She volunteers at the festival, and she'll be there from at least seven to midnight."

I stew on the information for a second. "What about Don?"

He considers my words, brows lifting. "He's more likely than Preston. As far as being inherently evil, anyway. I've never liked that guy. He's a pervert and basically lives off Joe. Does he have motivation, though?" He frowns. "I'm not sure he's even in Joe's will. Does Lexi know?"

"No. She only knows there's a paternity test in there, and that's the long and short of it."

He rubs his hand through his hair and then scratches the back of his head. "Mention it to Lexi and see what she says. She may have already considered and dismissed him for some reason—maybe since there's really no motivation for him to kill me."

"Okay, so who are our other options? Anyone that would kill you for money or love or hate?"

He widens his eyes. "Maybe Lexi murdered me for my hairbrush. She did also get some collectibles from *The NeverEnding Story*, and my *Beetlejuice* memorabilia."

I roll my eyes. "As intriguing as all that sounds, it doesn't seem likely she would kill you and then beg me to help her figure out who murdered you since she's the only one who found your death suspicious in the first place."

"Unless that's her angle." He shifts closer to me. "You should ask her."

A surprised chuckle leaves my mouth. "I should ask her if she murdered you? Really? Because she's just going to admit it if she did?"

"No, but if you tell her you conversed with my spirit and *I* think she killed me, I bet she'd get a real kick out of it."

I roll my eyes and shake my head.

Bob jumps up on the back of the couch and stares down at Grey, her tail smacking him in the shoulder. He reaches back to pet her and she lies down and purrs, eyes closing in ecstasy.

"It's so weird."

"What?" He glances over at me.

"Bob hates everyone but me."

He smirks. "And me. I'm very lovable. So, I guess we can scratch Bob off our list of potential suspects."

"If we're adding felines to the list, we've really reached the bottom of the barrel. You really have no enemies?"

"Nope."

I sigh. "I guess we keep looking in there then." I gesture to the books and then eyeball what's left. "Not too much more to go through. Looks like we're about halfway there."

His voice booms through the room. "Oohhh livin' on a prayer!"

I groan and cover my face.

"Stop it. Don't hide from me. You love it." He tugs my hands from my face, keeping them in his grip as our eyes lock and hold.

"I kind of do, actually."

His brows lift and heat rushes up my face.

"I mean, you're obnoxious, and if you steal my robe, I may have to kill you myself, but if I had to be stuck living near a time portal with a random dead guy, I'd pick you first."

"That's very sweet," he says, completely straight faced. "And if I had to pick just one paranormal heiress, it would definitely be you."

I laugh. "Are there any others to choose from?"

He grins. "I guess not." His gaze dips to my mouth, his smile dropping. His hands are wrapped around my wrists.

When his eyes flick back up and meet mine, they're full of heat—the same heat spreading through my stomach and making my limbs tingle.

Is he going to kiss me?

"Why the eighties stuff?" I blurt.

He blinks at the sudden question and releases me from his gentle clasp. "What do you mean?"

I swallow, my hands falling to my lap, twisting there. Maybe I shouldn't have stopped that moment. "I mean, the DeLorean, the Polaroid camera, singing the eighties songs, why are you into that decade specifically? I'm not knocking it, I'm just curious."

He reaches toward me, brushing a loose strand of hair that's escaped my ponytail, his finger brushing against the shell of my ear.

My breath catches, my pulse racing with the tenderness of the movement, my mouth dry.

"I think it started when I was a kid and I watched

that movie, *Real Men* with John Ritter and Jim Belushi?" His brows lift in question.

I blink through the mist of lust he's incited in me with a simple touch and shake my head. "I don't think I've seen it."

He shrugs. "Anyway, I really liked that movie. I watched it over and over and I always wished that John Ritter were my dad. He was a cool guy, and I don't know." His cheeks tinge pink. "It's probably stupid, but it was just something to focus on. Something to distract me from reality."

"I get that." I nod.

His eyes are intent on mine. "I know you do."

We stare at each other.

I lick my lips.

"Amelia," my name is a rough whisper.

"Yes."

He leans forward.

Bang, bang, bang.

We leap apart. My heart pounds, this time from fear.

"Amelia, I know you're home. Open up!"

His gaze shoots to mine. "That's Lexi."

"No one can see you here," I whisper.

We scramble off the couch, and I move toward the door.

She's yelling through the door. "I know it's kinda late, but I have news."

I keep my voice low. "You have to hide. She can't see you."

"But I want to hear what she has to say."

"Go to my room—stay out of sight."

He nods. "I will be right here, waiting for you," he whispers with a wink before sneaking down the hall.

I freeze, staring after him. "Wait, was that a Richard Marx song?" I whisper-yell.

He just gives me a thumbs up before disappearing inside my bedroom.

I shake my head, suppressing laughter before I open the door.

"Hey." Lexi is on my front porch in flannel pajama pants and a T-shirt, her hair in a messy bun on top of her head. "You're not going to believe this."

Chapter Sixteen

She stalks past me into the house.

"Come on in," I say when she's halfway to the kitchen.

She laughs. Bob flies out from the hallway and swipes at her before racing down the hall toward the bedrooms.

"Bob. Nice to see you, too," she calls.

In the living room, she stops. "It looks almost as sloppy as it did when Grey lived here."

"Oh, sorry. Let me move this stuff out of the way. I was uh, working." I hold up one of the journals and then stack a few of them together on the table.

Lexi glances around at the double plates and wine glasses. "Did you have company?"

"No." The word is a sharp bark.

She stares at me, brows lifted.

"I was really hungry." Before she can ask further, I

gather as many dishes as I can and scurry to the kitchen to dump the evidence in the sink. "So, what's going on?"

"I got the DNA results back."

"And?" I sit on the recliner across from her.

"Preston isn't Grey's brother."

I slump in the chair. "Oh. So maybe there is no motive for him. Maybe a paternity test in the file means something else or is about someone else."

She's already shaking her head. "There's more."

"What is it?"

"Grey's not his brother, but he is Preston's cousin. First cousin, from the looks of it."

"Cousin?" My voice escalates.

A muffled thump sounds from the recesses of the house.

Lexi straightens, glancing in the direction of the noise. "What was that?"

"Probably Bob. Let me go check." I stand.

"I'll come with you."

I hold up a hand to stop her. "No, it's fine."

"What if it's Grey, though?" she stage-whispers, eyes wide. "Have you seen him lately?"

"No, I haven't." It most definitely *is* Grey, but she can't see him like this. All alive and stuff. She'll freak. "Maybe you should just stay here."

Her eyes narrow. "Why? If it's nothing, then it shouldn't be a big deal for me to check it out with you." She leans back, eyes widening. "Are you hiding a man?"

She glances around and lowers her voice. "It's not Preston, is it?"

"What? No!"

She releases a breath. "Thank the heavens for that. I was about to stage an intervention. Maybe an exorcism."

"Fine. You can come with me." I raise my voice, hoping Grey can hear. "We can check out the noise together. Me and you. Lexi and Amelia."

Her brows furrow. "Why are you yelling about yourself in the third person? Have you been drinking? I mean, I can see you were double-fisting the wine glasses, but you're not acting smashed. Just weird." She shakes her head. "You've been cooped up here alone in this house for too many days."

"Fine, just—come on." I stomp toward the hallway and then take my time, loudly inspecting the office first, slamming the door and making a ruckus before we head to my bedroom.

"Nothing here."

"What about the closet?" She stalks toward it.

"What? No—!"

She swings the door open.

My shoulders drop. It's empty.

"It was just this flashlight." She bends down and picks it up, turning to face me, perplexed.

"Oh. It must have . . . fallen."

One eyebrow lifts. "That flashlight fell down and turned itself on?"

I shrug.

She nods with certainty. "I knew it. Grey was here." She lets out a forlorn breath. "But I guess he's gone now." She clicks off the flashlight and hands it to me.

She's not wrong.

Back in the living room, she sits on the couch and stares up at me, eyes wide. "If you ever happen to see or hear anything, and he ever has a message for me, would you . . ."

I sit next to her and put a hand on her arm. "Of course, Lexi." I bite my lip. "I can tell you one thing."

"What is it?" She sits up straighter.

"He loved you."

She rolls her eyes. "I knew that."

"You were his best friend. He considered you family."

She stares at me for a second, her eyes bright, and then her gaze drops to her lap.

"He also may have suggested you murdered him for his eighties memorabilia."

She bursts out laughing. Then she looks over at me, expression awed. "Yep. That sounds exactly like something he would say."

I bite my lip, uncomfortable with making her think I'm some kind of medium, even if the words themselves are true.

She huffs out a sigh and leans back on the couch. "So, I don't want to say it, but it's possible Don was Grey's dad."

Oh, right. Preston and Grey are cousins. Don and Joe were brothers, so that would make sense.

I nod, but the thought of the old smarmy playboy being Grey's biological father doesn't quite sit right. "That would fit. It would make them cousins, I guess."

She's shaking her head. "I can't imagine Bonnie with Don. He's such a slime. Bonnie was an angel. She was so sweet. He has a new girlfriend half his age every week."

"What are the other possibilities? Maybe Don is Preston's father?"

Lexi blinks. Leans back on the couch. "Claire and Don? And then . . . Joe and Bonnie?" She shakes her head and grimaces. "I don't know. That would be insane. But possible, I guess. You never really know what's going on behind closed doors."

We contemplate in silence for a few minutes.

"Are there any other Blake siblings?" I ask.

"No. Just the two of them."

"What about Grey's mom? Did she have any brother or sisters?"

"She had a sister, but she died years ago." She crosses her arms over her chest and then looks at me out of the corner of her eye. "There is a way we can confirm if Don is the dad."

My head shoots up in alarm.

She darts a glance at me. "There's a charity function next weekend at the Blakes'."

I wait but she doesn't speak further. "And?"

Her words come out in a rush. "You could easily get

Preston to take you. Then when you're there, get something of Don's we can test."

I groan. "Not this again."

"It should be easier, no fake bees needed. Don smokes cigars, so all you have to do is steal one after he's done with it."

"Right because no one will notice me playing in the trash."

She grins. "That's the attitude."

"Wait, what does this mean about Grey's death, though? Do you think the uncle had something to do with it? If he's Grey's father, that wouldn't change anything, right? Why would he kill his own son?"

She lifts her hands in the air. "I have no idea. I don't think Don would want the information getting out. Maybe Don didn't like that Joseph included his nephew in his will instead of him."

"Doesn't Don have his own money?"

"He has some, but Joe was more successful. Rumors are that Don blew most of his inheritance on women, booze, and bad investments. As far as I know, he wasn't in Joe's will at all."

"Because of Grey?"

She shrugs. "Maybe."

"But his death didn't change that, did it? There was nothing more in it for Don."

"Appears that way, but maybe he didn't know that. No one in town really knows what was in the trust except Claire, and she isn't sharing. Trusts are not public documents like wills are."

"So how is figuring out who Grey's dad is going to help us solve his murder?"

"I have no idea, but unless you're ready to try a séance right now, you got any better ideas?"

I blow out a breath. "How, exactly, am I going to get Preston to invite me to this thing?"

Lexi grins and then picks up my phone from the coffee table.

"What are you doing?"

"Just trust me." She taps out something and then hands me back my phone.

It's open to a text message that reads, "Are you busy this weekend?"

"Lexi!" The phone buzzes in my hand.

Preston is calling right back.

She snorts a laugh. "That was quick. Desperate much?"

I shoot her a dark scowl and then answer the phone. "Hey, Preston."

"Amelia. It's so nice to hear from you."

I grimace.

"I was very glad to receive your text."

Surprising, considering our last date, but like Grey said, Mystic Falls has slim pickings. "That's . . . great. I was happy to . . . send it."

Lexi quakes with silent laughter, one hand covering her mouth.

"I have plans this weekend, a family charity dinner to benefit the Wildlife Foundation."

"Oh, you have plans? That's fine then. Maybe some other—"

"Actually, if you're not busy, you could be my plus one? I know it's rather last minute, but since you were inquiring about my plans, and I'm sure you have a nice dress somewhere, something formal?"

"Oh, yeah. Right. Sure."

"I'll pick you up at seven thirty on Saturday."

"Sounds great." I hang up and glare at Lexi. "I hate you."

She's smug. "It worked though."

"Except now he thinks I'm into him. Despite smacking him and yanking out his hair."

"You could shit on his lawn, and he'd think you love him. The man is a self-serving egomaniac."

"Now you tell me." I groan, flopping my head back on the couch. "I have to be alone with him. What if he murders me?"

"He won't murder you. He's not the serial killer type, just the, you know, murder of convenience type."

"Your concern for my welfare is touching."

She laughs. "I'll wait for you here when he drops you off so I can collect the sample. At the event, you'll be surrounded by people. You can tell Preston I'm expecting you by a certain time. He's not an idiot. He'd be suspect number one if anything happened to you."

"Fine. Why aren't you going to this thing?"

She shrugs. "Not invited. Actually, officially unin-vited by my dad because he's sick of me talking smack to Preston all the time and he doesn't want me to make things 'uncomfortable' and say things that are 'inappro-priate.'" She rolls her eyes.

"So, he knows you."

"Pretty much, yes." She stands. "As much as I would love to turn this into a slumber party, I have to get some beauty sleep before work in the morning."

I walk her to the door, but before stepping out onto the porch, she turns and gives me a tight hug.

"Thank you for helping me. And for being a friend." She pulls back. "It's been a long time since I had someone I could talk to about anything. You know?"

"I do know." The urge to tell her the full truth slams into me. She might actually believe it. She doesn't doubt the ghost stuff or that I've seen Grey, but I hesitate. Is it fair to give her hope? If we don't get Grey through this, she might lose him all over again. "I've never had a real friend."

She squeezes my hand. "You do now."

After her car disappears down the drive, I check the house for Grey.

Maybe he's still here and he's just an exceptional hider.

Or maybe at some point, he returned.

Did he hear anything Lexi said?

"Grey?"

But one answers. He's gone.

I get ready for bed, my mind reeling with everything that's happened. It's all so surreal. Grey showing up and disappearing all the time, telling him about his death, reading through my parents' journals together, touching each other and talking like we've done it a million times before . . . the possibility that he was about to kiss me before Lexi interrupted us.

Was he going to kiss me? Does he feel the pull between us the same way I do? Why is everything so comfortable with him? I've never felt this way with anyone else.

What if . . . what if this isn't the first time we've been here? What if we've tried to save him before and we failed and the portal is giving us another chance? What if that's why he's so familiar?

So many questions and no real answers.

Does any of it matter? Do I have any control over anything?

I get into bed, sending one thought out into the universe.

Bring him back.

Chapter Seventeen

"Grey?"

I'm back in the in-between. The world is toneless. The air is thick. Heat surrounds me, the scent of orange and spice. A heart beats under my ear. I attempt to lift my head, but it's too heavy, my neck straining with the effort.

"Amelia?" An arm tenses around my waist.

I finally get my head up to meet his eyes. I'm lying on top of Grey, his arms around me, his eyes large and dark, his normally warm face gray and colorless.

He lifts a hand and stares at it, then puts it back around me, tugging me closer. "Don't leave."

"I'll try not to." The words are forced through thick vocal cords. He's like the only solid thing. Everything else is gelatinous and heavy, my brain fuzzy and foggy.

He slings a leg over my hips and I wiggle to get as close as possible.

We hold onto each other, the only substantial beings in a fuzzy land. My thoughts start to get sharper, clearer, more aware.

"Wait." My hands tense around his waist. "I think this is it. The place without colors. Why are we here? Did we change something?"

His fingers on my back move, his thumb rubbing in soothing circles. "I don't know. What could have changed?"

"I guess we'll find out."

I startle awake, jerking up in bed and glancing around the room. "Grey?"

The bed next to me is empty and cold, like it never happened. But it did, I know it.

It's been two days since I last saw Grey. What's changed? Why hasn't he come back?

Before loneliness has a chance to completely envelop me, something clangs in the kitchen. I strain, listening. Dishes clinking, pots and pans striking each other. The sounds have me scrambling up out of bed and racing to the kitchen.

He's whistling. A grin spreads across my face. I'm not sure, but it might be a Guns N' Roses song.

"You're here."

He's standing by the stove, wearing boxers and a white T-shirt, a spatula in one hand. "Hey." He smiles and memories of snuggling with him in bed come rushing back.

Pretty sure I rubbed my cheek against his chest like a cat. Flustered, I avoid eye contact.

But if he thinks I'm a freak, he doesn't let on. "Do you want some tea?" He motions to the kettle and tea bags and cups he's set out on the counter.

I walk over to it. The water is still hot. This confirms it. He's the perfect man.

"Did anything change?" I make my tea and then lean against the counter.

"What do you mean?"

"Do you remember? We were in that place. The colorless world like my dad wrote about."

"I remember." His eyes slide to mine. "I'm still dead. I already checked." He motions to my laptop, opened on the counter on the opposite side of the kitchen.

I slump.

"How do you like your eggs?" he asks.

"Oh. Um. Scrambled or whatever is fine. Whatever is easiest."

"Perfect." He turns back around to the stove, using the spatula to flip the potatoes. "I think we go there when even small things change—anything that affects a memory."

"Why do you say that?"

"The other night, when I went back to my time—by happenstance—Lexi was at my door, too."

"Really?"

"Yeah. She saw me in your robe. That was interesting to explain." He points the spatula at me.

"And yet I notice you aren't wearing my robe now, which means you took it into the past, so it must not have been that hard to explain since you decided to keep it."

He grins. "It's been two days. I had to wash it."

"What did we change the first time, I wonder?" I ask without thinking.

"First time?"

Oops. Maybe I don't want to remind him of the mutual orgasm that may or may not have been a dream. "I'll get the plates." I spin around and march to the cabinet.

"Wait. Amelia."

I grab the plates and turn around and can't go anywhere else because he's right in front of me, eyes bright in the morning light.

"That happened, didn't it?" His eyes search mine, intense and heated, and then his gaze dips down to where I'm clutching the plates. Or he's looking at my boobs. One of those things.

"It was because that was the first time I saw you," he says.

"What?" I blink. What is he saying? All I can think about is his gaze on mine, remembering his hands on my body, playing me like he was well acquainted with all my thoughts and every desire. The memory sends heat flooding to areas other than my face, lust spearing through me.

"I told Lexi about it."

My eyes widen. "You told Lexi about our sex dream?"

He smiles but tries to suppress it. "No. Of course not. I told Lexi I saw you in my house, not in my bed."

I want to run away and hide. My face is on fire.

Grey keeps talking. "I was—unsurprisingly—in the closet and everything kept changing. My clothes were there, then they were gone, then the door kept shutting seemingly by itself, and the light kept turning off. Then I saw you standing in the bedroom, staring at me. And then you just vanished."

"Okay." I take a deep breath. He didn't tell her about sex, he told her about the first time he saw me. "That makes sense. Yes. You told Lexi and it changed something. It changed her memories of the past, because before, that never happened."

Another thought strikes me like a bolt to the head and I reach out and grab his arm. "Wait. The first time Lexi told me she was suspicious about your death, she said you were seeing a figure in your house and stuff was moved. It was me. I'm who you saw. And because you saw me, and told her about it, that sole event triggered Lexi's suspicions. The first time I met her, before you saw me, she told me your death was an accident without even blinking. But we changed that and oh, my brain hurts now."

The food sizzles and pops on the stove and he spins away from me. He stirs the potatoes and flips the sausage. "It seems like every time I'm here, we change something. Which makes sense, because when I go back, I'm sure I'm not acting like I did before. Not after knowing everything I do now."

It's too bizarre to contemplate.

He cracks eggs into a bowl. "What did Lexi say the other night?"

"How long were you listening before you went back?"

"I heard that Preston isn't my brother, but he could be my . . . cousin?" He glances at me over one shoulder for confirmation.

I bring the plates over to the counter next to the stove. "Yep. You heard right. That's what the DNA results suggest."

His jaw clenches. "There's no way Don is . . . I can't even say it." He shakes his head, his eyes focused down on the food in front of him. "My mom couldn't stand him."

"I understand why you wouldn't want him to be related to you." I wince, thinking about how he was when I met him with Preston at the country club. "But we have to consider, maybe that's why she didn't want to tell you."

He shrugs and swallows. "I just can't picture them together. And even worse, what if it wasn't consensual?" He looks at me then, tortured. "I don't want to consider it."

I reach out, rubbing the back of his shoulder.

"Maybe not. Maybe he's not your father. We don't know anything for sure yet."

"I don't what other options there are if Preston and I are cousins and Don and Joe are the only possible fathers."

"Maybe Joe is your father, and Don is Preston's."

He shakes his head, brow furrowed. "I don't know. I can't imagine. None of it makes sense. Maybe there is a long-lost Blake brother out there somewhere that no one knows about."

"I'm going to get some DNA from Don this weekend. Lexi coerced me into accompanying Preston to a charity event at the Blakes', so we can compare his DNA to yours and Preston's. Maybe then we'll have more answers."

He nods, the motion jerky, and then pushes the eggs around with the spatula. "Or more questions. I'm not sure I want to know." He blows out a breath and then faces me. "Now let's eat and see if we can finish getting through those books."

"I think I found something." Grey reaches out, touching my leg just for a second.

I swallow, not wanting to think too long about how good his heat felt on my leg, how normal it is to touch each other, what it might feel like if he lingered, if his hand moved a little higher. I clear my throat. "What is it?"

He scoots closer so we can read the passage together, his entire side pressing into mine from shoulder to thigh.

His finger tracks down the page and then stops. "Here. 'Time is flexible and doesn't move in a straight line. There are different realities and the whole of it is too complex and incomprehensible to most. Only one thing is certain—the universe will move for love.'"

He stops and nudges me with his knee. "Well, that's romantic."

He keeps reading. "'The stars conspire to bring us our desires, to bring fated people together—be it lovers, friends, or family. The universe will show us our path. But we have to take the steps. Even fate can be thwarted by choice. Everyone has magic within them, but they have to believe it. Our own doubts and uncertainties, our failure to love that which is inside and out will deter what should be inevitable.'"

We stare down at the words together.

"Fated people," I murmur. "Constance. She had to live because without her, the Blake line died out." And if Grey is the son of Don or Joe . . .

"If your dad and Constance hadn't changed the past, I wouldn't be here."

I turn my head toward him, only inches away. Our gazes crash into each other. "What does it all mean?"

He considers me, eyes unreadable.

I swallow thickly.

"Amelia." His voice is gruff. He licks his lips and I track the motion, unable to look away.

I don't know who moves first. One second, I'm staring into his sleepy eyes, the next, his mouth is on mine.

My arms slide around his neck like we've done this before a thousand times.

And maybe we have.

Distantly, the book flops onto the rug. Bob lets out a disgruntled yowl and hops off the couch on the other side of Grey.

Grey leans into me and I move with him, sinking back onto the cushion. His hands are at my waist, his body pressing into me from above, a comforting, decadent weight. My hips fall open and he settles between my legs.

Only two layers of thin fabric separate his heat from mine. His hardness presses into the perfect spot, flooding me with a hunger more intense than I thought possible.

The hot satin of his tongue sliding against mine for the first time is a primal revelation.

I can't hold back the moan that erupts from somewhere deep inside. My hips move, a clumsy effort to get relief. Desire thrums through me, mimicking the beat of my pounding heart.

"Amelia." He wrenches his mouth from mine, breathing heavily. "Wait. We should talk."

I follow him as he pulls back, kissing his scruffy chin,

licking his neck. "No more talking." Was that my voice that just spoke like that, so thick with passion?

He moans and captures my mouth with his again, this time with less finesse and more urgency.

I tug his shirt up, craving his skin against mine. He pulls away only to rip the tee over his head. Then he's yanking my own shirt off before pressing back into me. We both moan at the contact. His hands move up from my waist, one heated palm cupping my breast, covered only in a demibra. His thumb rubs my nipple through the thin fabric, the motion a tender contrast to the intensity of his tongue plunging into my mouth. Heat pools in my stomach, lower, and I squirm against him helplessly, but it's not enough.

I run my hands down his smooth, muscular back and then grip his ass, pulling him into me harder, right where I need him the most.

He follows my lead, moving his hips with mine, his hardness thrusting against me, his thumb continuing its teasing.

Without warning, an orgasm rips through me, the pleasure an explosion of sensation, breaking me apart and then piecing me back together.

He rests his head next to mine, his breathing haggard. His hand still cups my breast gently, his body still pressing into me, while I try to remember how to function like a normal human being.

"Grey."

He pulls his head up to grin down at me. "Yes, Amelia."

Heat suffuses my face. I can't believe we just did that. In broad daylight. No dream state to use an excuse. "Did you . . ."

"Enjoy myself? Yes, I did. We should do that again as often as possible."

"No, no. I mean did you . . . you know, go?"

"No." Unconcerned, he pushes a strand of hair from my forehead, his eyes tracing over my face. He lies down next to me, fingers tracing patterns up and down my arm.

"Don't you want to . . . you know, have your turn?" Why is it so hard to ask this?

He lifts his head, resting it on his palm and looking down at me. "Sex isn't a quid pro quo. Watching you orgasm was one of the highlights of what may turn out to be my very short existence."

"Don't say that." I smack him on his bare chest, but I can't find the will to remove my hand from his flesh. Instead, I rub the back of my fingers over his nipples and watch with interest as they harden at the ministrations.

"Amelia," his voice is strangled.

"Yes?" I ask innocently.

He grabs my wandering hand in his. "I like you."

"I sure hope so after the last fifteen minutes. Okay, maybe it was five minutes, but it's been a while for me."

His hand squeezes mine. "It's been a while for me, too. But we should talk about all this."

"Okay. Talk." I take my free hand and brush it over his stomach, playing with the waistband of his boxers.

"I—" He gasps and the sound sends a rush of pleasure straight to my core. "I don't think I can talk while you're doing that." His voice is strangled.

"Okay, then don't talk." This is the best time I've ever had. I've never had this kind of effect on a man before, let alone a man as attractive and funny and warm as Grey. Most guys don't want to talk, they want to get what they want and leave.

"I don't want to disappear before we have a chance to discuss all of this."

The reminder that this is temporary, that it has to be, smothers the fire building in my gut. My hands still and he must read something in my face because his arms come around me and he holds me to his chest.

"I'm sorry."

"Why are you apologizing? You haven't done anything wrong. I was the one harassing you."

He chuckles, his chest shaking against my cheek. "You can't harass the willing."

His arms tighten around me, and I enjoy it for a few long moments, breathing in his scent, indulging in the strength of his arms wrapped around me like a cocoon of safety.

But it's not the real world. And despite what he inferred earlier—is this totally crazy to feel so much after so little time? We barely know each other. And it's not like it's a long-distance relationship because he lives in another county or even across the country. He's from a different *time*. And if it weren't for this strange time continuum thing, I wouldn't be able to see him at all because in my time he's not even alive.

This whole thing is banana hammock crazy.

After a while, I pull back to meet his eyes. "What now?"

"I'm not sure. I think I'm having an existential crisis. I feel like I've known you forever. There's this familiarity. Like I've known you a long time. Do you feel it, too?"

"Yes." I lift my hand to cup his cheek, his scruff scratching my palm. "But this would be a bad idea."

He leans down, running his nose down my neck and inhaling, igniting nerve endings and eliciting a gasp. "Terrible idea. Obviously." His breath is warm against my collar bone.

"Wait." I struggle to remember what we're talking about. "Why is this a bad idea?"

"Because . . . I'm dead?"

I run a hand down his front, cupping him through his shorts. "You don't feel dead."

He groans and his head drops to my chest. "Woman. You're really taking all my attempts at nobility and tossing them right out the window."

"I'll be good on one condition."

He pulls back to meet my eyes. "Name it. I surrender."

Chapter Eighteen

I bite my lip. "Can we not talk about dying or anything about the time loop? Just for a little bit? Just tonight, for now, can we just pretend, for as long as you'll be here, that we're just two people who like each other and are getting to know each other?"

He nods. "Yes. Fine. Tell me all your deep, dark secrets."

I laugh. "I don't have any of those. I'm boring. Actually, you are my biggest secret."

His eyes search mine. "While that might be true, I disagree about the boring part. You're anything but boring, but feel free to tell me all your most boring secrets."

"Okay. I can do that. My first boring truth is that I've never had a real boyfriend before." I can't look at him and make this confession. I'm twenty-five. It's so embarrassing.

But the words barely faze Grey. "That doesn't count. You already told me you can barely make it past a third date. This isn't a new secret. Unless . . ." His head tilts. "Are you trying to tell me you're a virgin?"

We're still lying on the couch together, facing each other. I'm on the inside, my back supported by the couch while he lies stretched out next to me. His hand plays with mine, resting on the couch between our bodies.

"Not a virgin." I laugh. "But I wouldn't say I'm experienced. I've had a lot of horrific dates and couldn't quite make it to the grand finale on most of them."

"Tell me about your worst date." He squeezes my hand.

"Let's see. There was the guy who made me listen to a jazz record for like an hour."

"The horror," he gasps. "That's it? That's your bad date story? Jazz music?"

"It gets worse. In the middle of the record, the music stopped and there were barnyard noises for like ten minutes before the jazz just started up again."

A surprised laugh burst out of him. "Are you serious?"

"I wish I wasn't. That was bad enough, but there's more. When it started, I of course was shocked so I looked over at him, and his eyes were shut like the music was still playing and it wasn't a bunch of pigs snorting and cows mooing."

He laughs, pulling our clasped hands against his

stomach, the muscles flexing under our fingers, his eyes almost shut in his mirth.

"That's the best thing I've ever heard."

"Your turn. You didn't disclose anything about past girlfriends even when I attempted to pry. Why is that?"

He shifts, reaching out to pick up a strand of hair that's fallen forward over my shoulder. He rubs it between his fingers. "I don't have any fun stories like you do. I didn't really date in high school. Then in college, I didn't have time for anything serious. I did go out a few times with a few different women, but nothing ever lasted longer than a month."

"Are *you* a virgin?"

He grins at me when I throw his question back at him. "Not a virgin."

"Any terrible date stories?"

"Nah, the women I went out with were normal, I guess, but there wasn't anyone that made me feel," he shrugs, "anything. You know?"

"Yeah." I nod. "Same."

Our eyes lock, his gaze glittering with sudden intensity.

"There was never anything," his hand trails up my arms, fingers leaving goose bumps in its wake, "like," he leans forward, breath puffing against my neck right before his lips brush the delicate flesh at my throat, "this."

I shudder, swallowing the rising tide of lust he incites with just a brush of his mouth.

He nips at my skin and then pulls back. "Maybe we should change the subject before this gets out of control."

"I don't see a problem with getting a little out of control." I squirm closer, sliding my leg between his.

"What happened to being good?"

I run a hand up his arm, over his shoulder, cupping the back of his neck. "Was that me who said that?"

His breath hitches in his throat. "I believe it was."

"That must have been someone from a different timeline."

He chuckles. "You're entirely too tempting."

"Really?" It's not a bait for compliments, but it sort of is. This whole thing has been surreal from the start, but now, having Grey's eyes on me and filled with lust and want and yearning—all of it mirrored in me—it's like some kind of fever dream.

He kisses me then, his hand spearing into the hair at my nape to hold me in place while his mouth plunders, destroying me for anyone else, ever.

After a minute, he pulls away and rests his forehead against mine.

"Tell me more things." His voice is rough with desire.

I swallow, taking a couple of breaths to slow my racing heart. "Like what?"

"When did you move to LA?"

"When I was seventeen."

"Seventeen? That young? Your parents didn't go with you?"

"No. I left them and—" If he wanted to slow down the need and lust building between us, this conversation is a good way to dim my desire. I shake my head. "We fought and I left. I had to go. The resentment had been building by that point for years and I just . . . shattered."

"When did you first realize it was a lie?"

I appreciate that he believes me. He doesn't question whether I was wrong, considering our present circumstances. Despite the fact that maybe they weren't *always* running a con, I know what I saw and I know a majority of their jobs were pure fiction, something they used to make money.

"I was about fourteen."

At first, they only faked it when we really needed money. They made a little on the real stuff. My mom would do palm readings, tarot, whatever. But it wasn't always enough, and her gifts weren't always consistent.

I pull back to meet his eyes. "My dad had a heart problem, so when he needed to pay for his medication, or the truck broke down, or a client stiffed us, they would scam people, just enough for a bit of cash. It was only supposed to be until they could break even on things. But once they started making more money, they a hard time stopping."

His thumb rubs a soothing circle on the back of my neck, relaxing the muscles tensing there.

"They helped people. That's how they would spin it.

They were the good guys. They gave people peace and closure. They made me feel like I was a part of something bigger than myself."

I glance down, a memory rising. "Then one time they were doing a walk-through on a case. Dad distracted the couple in the kitchen, and Mom . . . she was in their bedroom, reading a diary. She didn't see me, but I watched her flip through someone's personal thoughts. The couple had lost a child, you see. When my mom did their 'reading' later, she knew things—not things she discerned with her gifts. Things she knew because she had snooped."

I snort. "After that, I couldn't stop seeing it. Everywhere we went, they used the same tactics. Mom would use her ability when she could, but whatever she didn't know, they would find by snooping in people's houses. And worse."

Or maybe it just got worse once I noticed. To convince people they were legit, they'd pretend to see things moving out of the corner of their eyes. They'd mess with cable jacks to add static on recordings and then swear it was someone whispering, "help me," or "I'm here."

"Once they embraced social media, Mom basically stopped relying on her gift entirely, stalking people on social media for fodder instead."

He nods. "They used suggestibility."

"Exactly. At first, I tried to not think about it. I thought maybe it was okay. I mean, we would leave families better off than when we arrived. It helped them, even if it was fake. But after a while I just needed to get out."

"Why did you decide to go to LA?"

I shrug. "Not sure. I had no idea what I wanted with my life. I just wanted to be away from my parents. I guess I liked the idea of a big city full of people with dreams, being able to disappear into something bigger than myself. I got a job waitressing at a fancy restaurant on Sunset Boulevard while I did some freelance writing jobs in my spare time. I enjoyed writing but never thought it would be anything worthwhile or a way to make a living."

I take a deep breath and then blow it out before continuing. "My parents called me before they died. They were going to a job outside San Diego. They asked me to join them, but I said no. We fought again, and that was the last time I talked to them."

A lump grows in my throat, my eyes tingling. The guilt chokes me into silence.

"How did it happen?"

I swallow. "They were with someone else, one of their clients, and he was driving. They think he might have been on drugs or under the influence of something. He crossed a double line and drove them straight into a truck coming the other way."

His arms tighten around me. He presses his lips to my forehead and whispers against my skin. "I'm so sorry, Amelia."

I swallow through the pain threatening to pull me under and keep going.

I can't tell him what happened next, how I went off the rails, trying to escape the guilt and shame. I spent more nights than I care to remember drinking. I lost the waitressing job. I lost my virginity. All I cared about was forgetting.

"Six months after they died, I hit rock bottom. I didn't have enough money for rent. I was about to be homeless. I had been writing some freelance stuff, and I wrote and published a story about my parents. I didn't write it for the money, though. I wrote it for me. It was cathartic. It was a release."

His free hand finds mine and links our fingers, squeezing. "You don't have to talk about it."

"I want to. It was just one story among many, one of the cases I remembered the most because it was terrify- ing. A man had killed his whole family in this house in New Jersey. The new owners were sure it was haunted. One of their children was acting possessed. The story had everything they loved. My parents fixed it. Fixed their house, cured the kid, and made them feel safe in their home."

He lifts my hand to his mouth, brushing his lips against my wrist. "You wanted to remember the good parts."

I nod. "I didn't think anything of it when I posted it online. I had written articles before that no one ever saw. Publishing it was just like putting a piece of them out into the ether, a way to assuage my guilty conscience. But then it went viral. It just took off."

I clench my back teeth together, remembering. "And then I was being offered all this money if I could tell more of their stories. I just had to sell the rights to their lives and mine. And I did it. I used the reason I left them, the very thing I reviled—I turned around and used it to make money."

My throat closes up. I can't go on. I can't believe I've verbalized as much as I have—things I've thought and never actually spoken out loud. I can't meet Grey's eyes. I can't look at him and witness judgment or derision.

His arms tighten around me, and he tugs me into his chest. His arms surround me with warmth as he just holds me without demand or censure. It's the only thing that allows me to continue.

"And even worse, I didn't go to them, even when they asked. Even when they begged. And if I had . . . would they still be alive?"

He holds me tighter. "It's okay to feel bad. It's not your fault."

The tenderness in his voice is what pushes me over. The tears spill out, soaking his chest, but he just continues to hold me, one hand rubbing my back in soothing circles, his cheek resting against the top of my head.

Time passes, but eventually the tears subside. I gather my composure enough to pull away from him.

"I'm sorry." I can't meet his eyes.

"Nothing to be sorry for. It's okay to feel however you feel."

"I got you all wet."

"I'll dry. If you feel even a little bit better, it's worth a few tears on me. Even some snot."

A surprised laugh escapes me, and I finally meet his eyes. "I just wish I could go back and tell them."

His gaze is warm and soft, as comforting as hot chocolate. "What would you say?"

"That I loved them anyway. Even though I was angry, even though I left . . . they were still my parents."

"I'm sure they knew. They loved you."

"You can't know that." My voice breaks.

He rubs my back again and then dips his head to meet my eyes. "I fought with my mom before she died, too."

I blink away the remnants of tears. "You did?"

"None of us gets through the death of a loved one unscathed. I still feel guilty about every fight I had with my mom, every day. Especially the last one. It was the week she died. She told me she wanted to talk to me about something, and I didn't want to wait. I wanted her to tell me whatever it was over the phone. But she insisted we have the talk in person. I shouldn't have pushed her, but I can't go back and change it now."

I squeeze him a little tighter.

"Like you, I sort of went crazy after she passed. I went traveling. Disappeared for a while. I needed to forget everything. I was just lost. I finally came home because I realized she wouldn't have wanted me to throw my life away in regret. She would have wanted me to live. To be happy. Your parents loved you. They wouldn't want you to suffer. Let me show you something." He rolls away, off the couch and over to the stack of books we've already sorted through.

I push myself up to sitting while he digs through the box. "I read this earlier . . . ah, here it is." He moves back over and sits next to me, flipping through the book to find the page.

"Here." He points. The journal entry is dated March 2011, only a few months before they died. "'When Amelia was young, we used to tell her the story of how we first met—how I knew the moment I laid eyes on her mother that she was the one for me. I was in darkness, and my Meredith was the sun.'"

I smile. "He did say that all the time. It was so cheesy. One thing I never doubted was their love for each other. He looked at her like she'd invented the Ouija board, and she was just as bad."

He chuckles and then keeps reading. "'What I never told her, what I should have said, was that if Meredith was my light, Amelia was my air. Together, they are all I need for life. It's hard to breathe without her, but I know she has her own wings to stretch, her own light to find, her own darkness to contend with.'"

I guess I'm not all cried out because the tears resurface, spilling onto my cheeks.

Grey tugs me into his side. "I'm sorry. Maybe I

should have shown you this sooner, but I thought you knew."

"No. I didn't know. It's fine. Thank you for finding this. For showing me."

"He loved you a lot," Grey says, his voice low and somber.

"I guess he did." The pain is sharp, a lance to the heart. "I was so cruel." I sniff. "And then they died."

I wipe at my cheeks and Grey picks up the throw blanket on the back of the couch and mops my face with it, making me giggle.

"Enough of this," I tell him, blowing out a breath. "I wish I could go through that damn portal and back to when they were still alive."

"So, what you're saying is, you'd like to . . . turn back time." His eyes are wide, alight.

I point at him. "Don't do it."

He throws his head back and belts into the air, "If I could turn back time . . ."

"Stop!" I cover his mouth with my hand before he can continue and then Bob takes that moment to yowl into the air.

She's still on the recliner, staring at us, ears twisted back, and then we're laughing, and somewhere in between the laughing, we're kissing again.

It's like once we start, we can't stop. The inferno erupts.

We end up stretched out on the couch again, him on

top, cradled between my legs, and then he pushes himself up and looks down at me.

"I want to be clear that I like you."

I lift my brows and run my gaze up and down his torso, what's visible between my legs. "I get that."

"No. It's more than physical. I don't do temporary affairs or one-night stands. I've wanted you from the moment I saw you."

"Really? From the moment you saw me and thought I was a poltergeist?"

He grins. "Actually, it was the second I realized you were messing with me. I don't think I've ever been so fascinated. I never would have imagined meeting a woman who would pretend to be a demonic orphan who lives in a well. It was beyond creative."

I roll my eyes. "You laughed at me."

"It was impressed laughter. Honestly, that was the moment I thought to myself, she might be the one."

The laugh dies in my throat. The one?

His eyes are earnest, searching mine, but there's tension around his mouth, apprehension about how I'm going to respond to his words. "It's more than simple lust with us, at least it is for me. Does that freak you out?"

I swallow and shake my head. "No."

We stare at each other for a hot, tangled second, and then we're kissing, gasping, groaning, limbs entwining.

"I want you," I tell him when I pull back to take a breath. "Wait. Do you have any condoms?"

He blinks down at me, expression dazed with lust. "Shit. I didn't stash any under the floorboards when I lived here. What is wrong with me?" His voice is so full of self-recrimination, I burst out laughing.

"You better remedy that."

He nods. "Trust me, I will. There's a loose floorboard in the closet. I'll stick a box in there for next time."

"Oh, yeah. The secret compartment where Dad found the original murder article. I've searched that whole closet. I haven't found it."

"It's hidden in the corner. You wouldn't see it unless you pulled up on the board a specific way. I'll show you. In the meantime, where we're going, we don't need roads."

"What?" I laugh.

He doesn't respond, his gaze sliding down my body along with the rest of him. He doesn't make it far, stopping at my chest to worship one breast and then the other until my legs are squirming together and I might die if he doesn't move further south.

"Grey." His name is a tortured moan.

Like he can read my thoughts and therefore every want and need, he moves, tugging my shorts down as he goes, along with my panties, tossing them aside. His hands tighten on my thighs, spreading them wider as his dark head settles between my legs.

"You're so perfect." His hot breath blows over me, his words a feral growl. "I'm going to enjoy this."

My hands clench against the couch, anticipation a drum beat pounding throughout my body. An eon passes before he finally leans in and brushes his lips against me.

Air staggers in and out of my lungs.

His mouth is a slow, smooth press, brushing up and down over and over.

I'm panting, squirming, ready to grab his head and make him push harder, and that's when his tongue comes out and flicks against me.

I gasp, shuddering as his tongue continues, running up and down in an unhurried sweep before delving straight into my core. My back arches, pressing closer to his face, but he's not in any hurry. He continues a slow slide, up and down, pausing only to flick his tongue against the bundle of nerves at the top and then sliding back down, repeating the motions, pressure increasing with each sweep.

When I think I'm going to explode into a release, he withdraws.

A groan escapes me. "Don't stop. If the universe takes you away before I orgasm, I'm going to be so pissed."

He moves back in, his laughter rumbling against my core, the vibration surging me back to the pinnacle of pleasure.

His attention narrows, tongue flicking against me and then following it up with gentle sucks. One thick finger presses into me, and that's all it takes to push me over the edge I've been teetering on. I come hard and fast around him, hands pressing against his shoulders, an attempt to anchor myself to the moment, to him, to the pleasure ricocheting through me.

I collapse back on the couch, limp and loose. Grey moves next to me, tugging me onto his bare chest. His arousal is a brand of heat against my bare skin—even through his boxers. We lie together, catching our breath, his heart racing under my ear.

"Wow," he says finally.

My fingers trace down his chest, stopping at the elastic waist of his boxers before sneaking under the waist band and grabbing him in my hand.

"Yeah, wow." I stretch toward him, kissing his neck, sucking on the delicate skin there. "It's my turn to play."

He sucks in a gasp, breathing unsteadily. "I'm not going to argue this time. But I am going to warn you, I already told you it's been a while since I've done anything with a woman and I'm already—" He blows out a breath. "You're already, uh—" He swallows.

"I'm not judging. I doubt you can come faster than I did."

"I wouldn't make that bet." His eyes brand me with the heat in them.

Grinning, I slither over his body, tugging his boxers down just enough to pull his length out and hold it in my grip.

He watches me, eyes glittering in the low light, lust a palpable thing between us.

Then I lick him.

He gasps and his hands clench at his sides.

"You can touch me," I whisper against the head of his cock before sucking it into my mouth.

"Oh, holy hell, Amelia." My name on his lips is a plea and a curse all rolled into one.

I draw away to smile up at him, then pull him back into my mouth. Licking, sucking, teasing with my tongue, my mouth, my hands until finally he moves.

His hands hover around my head.

I reach my free arm up and push his hands onto my hair.

It's like he was waiting for that moment, that encouragement and permission, because with a heavy groan, his fingers tighten on my head and his hips jerk up. I open wide, letting him take what he needs until he explodes in my mouth. I relish every shudder, every drop of bliss quaking through his body, like his ecstasy is mine.

We collapse together on the couch, Grey on his back, me splayed out on top of him.

"I think you killed me. I don't die on Halloween, I die here. Death by pleasure."

I tap him on the chest. "That's not funny."

"But what a way to die."

He's warm, solid, and stable and holding him is like

coming home. But unless we can change the past, I can't keep him. I can't keep this.

If we do save him, what if he forgets? What if I forget? Is this all we'll have, a fleeting glimpse of what life could be? Something that might vanish even with victory? Even if we win, we could still lose.

Chapter Nineteen

"Amelia, it's wonderful to see you. You look great." Preston is right on time for our date that's absolutely not a date. His eyes flick up and down my dress, but it's not an appreciative male gaze checking me out because he's interested. It's more like he's making sure I've dressed suitably and he won't be embarrassed to be seen with me.

Apparently, I pass muster.

The dress is a deep red, off the shoulder, mermaid-style gown. Colleen helped me pick it out before a dinner I attended with the film company that purchased the movie rights to my story. I've only worn it once.

"Thank you. You look quite nice yourself." It's the lamest delivery in the world, but he beams.

And he does look nice. I mean he's well dressed, handsome, all the parts are in the right spot, but when he leans in to kiss me on either cheek—and this time I know it's coming so it's a lot smoother—I have to hold back the impulse to shudder.

Is it because Lexi thinks he's a murderer and my perception is tainted? Is it because I don't want anyone's lips on me but Grey?

He blathers on about his family's charitable contributions and how much work they do for the town for the entire drive. I barely get a word in edgewise, which is fine. If all I have to do is murmur incoherently, nod, and smile all night, it'll make my life a lot easier.

I use the time to think about Grey. How I haven't seen him in two days, but it feels like months. We spent a whole day together, talking about everything and nothing, touching each other, feeding each other, napping together, like we've been doing it for years. Until he disappeared, and I haven't seen him since.

Missing him is a persistent ache.

The Blakes' home is larger than I could have imagined. I knew they were rich, but I didn't know they were "faux castle, gated estate, immaculately maintained acres of grass and pond in the back" rich.

"Wow. It's beautiful." Lights blaze everywhere, shining up onto the grey stone and brick of the house itself—if it can even be called something as pedestrian as a house—and smaller lamps illuminate the landscaping, set up under bushes and trees.

Instead of driving around the circular drive to where valets take people's keys and park cars, he takes a road off to the side, leading to the rear of the house where he parks outside of a separate unattached garage.

I get out of the car before he can come around to open the door.

"We'll go in though the family entrance." He motions for me to follow him toward the house.

"What's that over there?" I point to a building on the other side of the pond as we make our way over the wide expanse of pavers and toward the mansion.

"It's the guest house."

The guest house is larger than any actual house I've ever lived in.

"Is that where Grey and his mom lived?" I ask.

There's a heavy pause. It's possible he didn't know that I knew about all that. Oops.

"Yes," he says finally.

"Who lives there now?"

"No one. It's been empty for years."

"It must be hard since Bonnie and Grey lived there for so long and now they're both gone." So maybe my prying is obvious, but I don't really care.

He opens the door for me. "She was like a mother to me." His voice is low, his mouth pressed into a thin line. The response doesn't seem feigned.

"I'm sorry for your loss." We walk together down a wide and quiet hallway, my heels clicking on the marble floor.

"It was worse for Grey. He was never quite the same after she died."

"I would imagine not."

Strains of violins and piano music whisper through the air. Where is the music coming from? I glance around and up. There are speakers, small unobtrusive circles, nearly blending in with the barrel vault ceiling.

"After she died, he took off, you know? He was just gone for almost two years. When he came back, I thought he was better. Not over it—you can never completely move on when a loved one dies—but like he was learning to live with the loss. But then—" He clears his throat and glances around.

"But then what?"

"Toward the end, before his accident, he was acting really off."

I stop walking. That is the exact opposite of what he said before. "He was? That's not what you said when I asked."

Preston stops and faces me, brows furrowed in confusion. "What do you mean?"

"When we had brunch together, you said he was perfectly normal and you hadn't noticed him behaving out of the ordinary. I specifically asked if he was acting strange."

His frown deepens and then he shakes his head. "You must be mistaken."

He opens a door, and we step into the foyer. We've made it to the front entrance of the house where Claire and Don are greeting guests, like it's a receiving line at a wedding or something. Everyone is dressed and pressed in an array of colorful ball gowns and black and white tuxedos.

My jaw drops. The entry is enormous. Gleaming marble floors, a double staircase curving up into the second floor, a giant chandelier way high above glittering in the center of it all, the icing on the entire spectacle.

I don't have much time to process our conversation or the opulence around me because Preston leads us over to his mother and uncle.

"Amelia, so kind of you to join us this evening." Claire is impeccably dressed, makeup noticeable but muted. Her satin dress is white and long, topped with a matching jacket with ruffled sleeves. Her cane is matching ivory with jewels embedded in the handle.

Uncle Don is beside her in a black and white tux. Don's biggest accessory is a blonde plastered to his side in a short, teal dress. She's almost an exact replica of threesome Betsy: young, tan, and beautiful. They could be twins except for the hair color.

We shake hands. Preston kisses his mother, exchanges words with his uncle, and I try to maintain a smile.

Preston doesn't remember what he told me because Grey and I keep changing the past.

It had to be Grey finding out that Preston could be his cousin.

He must be acting strange toward Preston when he goes back to his own time, and now Preston remembers that whole sequence of events differently than he did just a few days ago.

"Would you like a drink?"

I snap back to the present. "Yes, please." Maybe twelve.

"We have a lovely Perrier Jouet Belle that is absolutely to die for."

I have no idea what he's talking about, but I nod and smile like a bobblehead and follow him into the ballroom.

I shouldn't be surprised considering the rest of the house, but it's an actual freaking *ballroom*. The white marble floors are inlaid with gold. The walls are golden. White wall sconces cast ambient light while another chandelier twinkles overhead. An entire orchestra plays on a raised platform off to one side, the musicians in black and white dresses and tuxedos. Holy cow. A wide-open dance space next them them is currently empty of dancers as revelers move around the rest of the space, grasping champagne glasses from circling waiters, or sitting around the tables covered in white tablecloths and gold utensils. The centerpieces are white flowers, green stems the only touch of real color in the whole place.

I try to remain cool. I have to focus on my goal here: get Don's DNA. I scope out his current location, where he's still shaking hands and kissing cheeks.

Okay.

I just have to make it through dinner and keep track of where he goes to smoke. I can do this.

Preston hands me a champagne flute full of sparkling liquid and I spend the next half hour with him introducing me to a myriad of people whose names I will never remember. All look vaguely bored and completely uninterested in meeting me.

Except for one person.

"Amelia, finally. Lexi has told me so much about you. I'm Sandra." Lexi's mom takes my hands in hers and squeezes, her smile wide and genuine and exactly like her daughter's.

Her husband is next to her. After exchanging greetings with Preston, he shakes my hand and says, "Lovely to see you again."

"You'll have to come over for dinner sometime soon," Sandra says.

"I would like that."

One of the waitstaff stops to say something low to Preston and he excuses himself and my shoulders slump in relief.

"Having a good time?" Sandra's smile is small and mischievous, her eyes twinkling at me.

"Oh, yeah. Great time." Wait. Did Lexi tell her what I'm doing here?

The music shifts and Mr. Stone leans into his wife. "Shall we dance?"

"No one else is dancing."

"We should start the trend." He holds a hand out.

She takes it and gives me a sheepish look. "I can never say no to this man."

They sweep onto the dance floor, some kind of waltz, I think, their eyes only on each other.

I wish I could dance with Grey. For a second, I allow the fantasy to take hold, his hand in mine, his arms around me. He'd probably crack some joke to make me laugh.

After a moment, a few other couples join them on the dance floor.

I walk slowly through the crowd of people, half listening to the murmur of conversation around me while scanning the rest of the room. Preston is clear on the other side, talking to a group of men in suits. Don is standing next to a table conversing with a couple of men while Claire sits in one of the chairs at his elbow. His date is nowhere to be seen. He grabs two glasses of champagne from a passing waiter and downs the first one and then the other in quick succession. His friends laugh. I roll my eyes and continue my stroll around the outskirts of the ballroom, sticking to the shadows.

"They're just continuing his legacy. You know how Joe was with philanthropy," a woman in a dark blue dress says.

"More like philandering," a second woman replies, and the group of women titters.

I halt and pretend to be engrossed in a particular section of wall that's exactly like every other section of wall.

"Ellen, it's not polite to speak ill of the dead."

"Besides," another voice chimes in, "the stories

about Joe were only rumor and conjecture. He never made a spectacle of his proclivities."

There's a moment of silence and I peek over my shoulder at the group of impeccably dressed women. There are five of them, ranging in age from midforties to probably late seventies. They all glance toward Don almost simultaneously, censure clear in every straight set of shoulders.

"Joe was nowhere near as bad as his brother."

"Don was always trying to live up to Joe, and he fails even in this."

More chuckles.

"Did you see what Cynthia is wearing?"

"Didn't she wear that same dress to last month's regatta gala?"

Ugh. I keep moving, mind working over what I overheard. So, there were rumors of Joe cheating on Claire. Maybe they were baseless, but sometimes even the most outlandish rumors have a root in something true.

The band segues into a slower song and Preston appears at my shoulder.

"There you are. Dinner is about to be served."

The music must be some sort of cue because everyone moves simultaneously, heading for their designated seats.

Preston guides me to our table, near the front, of course. We're sitting with Claire, Don, his woman of the hour, and a couple of the older men he talked to earlier.

Dinner is torture, tedious and lengthy torture. Plate after plate with one or two tiny bites.

I could really use a burger.

Through it all, Don drinks champagne and requests whisky from the waiters, mainlining booze like they might run out. His speech gets more and more slurred as the dinner wears on.

Through it all, Claire ignores him and makes chit chat with the rest of the table. She gets Preston to talk about one of his busines ventures, asks me about how I'm settling in, and even includes Don's date in a conversation about the weather.

Finally, the meal ends and Don gestures to one of his friends. "You have enough of those Arturo Fuentes to go around?"

His friend nods, and the group of men stand as one, heading toward the front doors.

This must be it. Here's my chance.

I wait about five minutes and then excuse myself to powder my nose.

Claire grips her cane. "May I accompany you? I need to stretch my legs a bit."

Dammit. I hesitate for a split second. I can't say no, though, can I? "Absolutely."

Claire stands, leaning on her cane, and guilt twists through me. She really does just need someone else to lean on. I make my way to her side and she takes my arm, offering me a relieved smile.

"Thank you so much, Amelia."

She points out how to get to the bathroom and we walk in measured steps—in the opposite direction from where Don and his cronies went.

What if I'm too late? What if I never find where they went? What if I do, and all five of those men toss their cigars in the same place? How will I ever know which one is Don's?

I take a slow breath, attempting to quell the impatience rising through me.

"Thank you for this. When the weather gets cooler, my arthritis acts up. Sometimes it's a struggle just to get out of bed."

Shame eats at me for wanting to dump her on the Aubusson rug we're treading over and run outside to hunt for cigars. "I'm happy to help."

We finally reach the bathroom, which is unlike anything I've seen in someone's home. It's more like a ritzy hotel restroom with a large mirror and lighting, a chaise lounge and sofa near one mirrored wall and doors that span from floor to ceiling for each toilet stall.

I'm helping Claire sit on the chaise when one of the doors opens and Sandra emerges.

"Amelia, Claire." She nods and smiles.

I escape into one of the stalls and let my anxiety pee out. When I emerge, Sandra is sitting on the chaise lounge alone.

"She's in the stall," she tells me, her voice low. "I'll

take her back to the ballroom if you need a minute." She winks at me.

Oh. *Oh.*

"Thank you. That would be nice."

She glances over at the doors and then says, "They're smoking over by the pond. I'll try and keep Preston from searching you out, but I don't know how much time you'll have." She squeezes my hand. "Good luck."

I exit the bathroom and decide to go out the side entrance where Preston and I came in, since it's the route I'm familiar with.

The pond is out behind the house, so I head in that direction.

At first, I worry about being spotted, keeping away from the light as much as possible. I pull off my heels, holding them in the same hand as my little clutch purse to quiet my steps.

I needn't have worried about it. The men are noisy enough to cover any of my movements, their voices strident in the dark night, their loud chatter interspersed with manly chuckles and guffaws.

Peeking around the corner of a bush, I review their locations. Their backs are to me, facing the water. I can't quite tell who is who, though, since they're all dressed in tuxes.

I need to get closer. There's a tree about ten paces in front of me. I could hide behind the wide trunk but getting there would leave me temporarily exposed. If one of them happens to turn around . . .

I have to risk it.

"Do you even know what to do with that woman you brought tonight?"

"This ain't my first rodeo, boys."

They laugh. I use the moment to make my way across the open space, aiming for the tree, my heart pounding. I press my back against the bark to catch my breath before peeking around the trunk. Thin tendrils of smoke float around them.

Phew. I'm not too late. Now I just have to see which direction Don tosses his cigar.

"It's a good thing you have her to take home and not Claire. You'd need extra Viagra for that one."

I wince. Gross.

"Don't talk about Claire that way," Don practically snarls.

Wow. Maybe he's not a total slimeball.

But then he continues. "I'm betting on my date drinking so much champagne she won't be able to talk tonight, and then tomorrow she won't be able to walk straight."

Whomp, there it is.

The other men chuckle and I try not to gag.

Is it a far stretch from date rape to murder?

The men finish their cigars. I squint into the darkness, focusing on Don.

A couple of the men put theirs out in a nearby flower pot. One man chucks his into the pond.

Oh, no. Please don't throw it into the water.

Thankfully, Don tosses his into the nearest bush and I release a relieved breath.

I wait until they've moved away, their voices disappearing into the distance, and then hustle over to the bush.

It's thick and shadowed with leaves. Despite the surrounding garden lights, it's impossible to see anything but leaves and branches and even those are hard to make out.

I pull my cell phone out, turning on the flashlight and pointing it inside the shrub, but it's too thick.

Dropping my heels on the grass, I crouch down and peer inside and underneath, shining my light around.

Nothing.

Dammit. I have to get into this thing. There's a small bit of space underneath. It's a large bush, clearly trimmed and maintained, but it's fall, so some of the leaves are molting faster than their landscapers can keep up.

I slide down on my belly and army crawl into the bush. I'm getting dirt all over my dress, and my updo keeps getting caught in branches, but I can't worry about that now. I shine my light on the ground and up in the bush around me, searching, searching, heart pounding.

Finally, my eyes alight upon the cigar butt. It's not on the ground, it got caught up above in a thick part of the branching. I almost missed it. I grab the baggie from my clutch and then reach up and pluck the cigar from the branch. "Gotcha."

"What are you doing under there?"

I freeze.

Shit. It's Preston.

Chapter Twenty

"I'm, uh," quick, *think, Amelia, think*. "Peeing!" The word shoots out of my mouth, loud and booming. Did it actually echo around the estate? Or was that just in my mind?

Killing the cell phone light, I somehow manage to shut it all up in my clutch.

"There is a bathroom inside," he says slowly.

I shove down a swell of hysterical laughter. "Right." I need to get out of this bush, with Preston watching.

This is not going to be pretty.

I back out, which is a lot of wiggling and straining and continuing to get my hair tangled in the branches.

By the time I've slithered out, my dress is covered in dirt and my hair is probably a nightmare. I swipe at myself a couple times and then stand up straight and meet Preston's gaze head on.

"The bathroom, it was, uh, really busy." Lame. So so lame.

He stares at me for a few long seconds and then bursts out laughing.

Heat climbs into my face, warming me despite the chill in the air.

"Amelia," he says when he's caught his breath. "Would you like to be just friends?"

My mouth pops open "What?"

"I know you're not into me. I get it, okay? I didn't think you'd want to crawl under bushes to get away from me, but it's fine. Honestly, I only asked you out to begin with because my mom was worried about you. It's hard to be new in town, and when people were talking about you, she felt bad. She gets that more than most. You don't have to be all . . . hiding in bushes and using Lexi as a shield."

"I, uh, don't?"

"Uh uh. And no offense or anything, but you're not my type. So, friends?" He sticks out his hand.

Is this a trick? Some kind of way to lull me into a false sense of complacency before the murder happens? I eyeball him, but he's relaxed, grinning.

I blow out a breath and shake his hand. "Friends."

"Would you like a ride home? I'm sure you don't want to explain to everyone else how you got your dress dirty while looking for a place to squat."

"Yes. Please." Tension bleeds out of me, leaving exhaustion in its wake.

The drive home is like a whole new experience. The pressure is off and we're both a lot more relaxed.

"Has everything been going okay with the rest of the people in town?"

I want to pick the leaves out of my hair, but I don't want to dirty Preston's pristine car more than I already have, so I keep my hands around the clutch in my lap. "Not really. Some teenagers toilet papered the tree in the front of the house last weekend."

He winces. "Hopefully this dinner will help smooth your way into at least some of the town's good graces."

"Yeah, I hope so. Lexi and her family have been kind, and you and Claire, too."

He clicks on the turn signal, slowing down to head up the gravel driveway to the cabin. "I'm glad you and Lexi are friends."

Shock has me leaning back into the leather seat. "You are?"

His eyes are fixed on the winding road in front of us. "I know she hates me, and maybe she has a good reason to." He shrugs, taking a second to glance over at me. "She was always a good friend to Grey. She's still sticking up for him and he's not even here."

I pause, thinking, wondering how much he's figured out about Lexi's clandestine investigation, wanting to ask more about what happened between them. I know Grey's side, but not Preston's. Not really.

"You and Grey were close, too."

He nods. "We were best friends as kids, more like

brothers than anything. And then as we got older and more competitive, about school, girls, sports, you name it, something changed. And it was mostly my fault."

"Why do you say that?"

"Because he was—" He cuts himself off. "I—I don't know. You know how hard it is to be a teenager, let alone being constantly compared to someone you can't quite measure up to, and he was younger than me."

He pulls the car to a stop in the driveway behind Lexi's Porsche SUV.

She's standing in the dark, leaning against the back of her trunk, arms crossed. Her car is running, the headlights shining into the trees. The porch lights are still on, casting gobs of golden light onto the front of the house and halfway up the property.

"Speak of the devil."

"Oh, right. Yeah, Lexi's here. Uh, she just came to pick up a thing, a book I promised to loan her." I'm the worst liar.

He nods and doesn't question further.

"Thank you," I tell him.

He nods. "Have a good night."

I wave at his dark vehicle, unable to see if he waves back before he reverses and drives away.

Lexi pushes off the car as I approach. I glance behind me before opening my clutch, making sure he's out of sight even though the sound of spitting gravel has ebbed.

I hold out the plastic wrapped object.

"Is that the cigar?"

I roll my eyes. "No, it's a velociraptor."

Lexi bursts out laughing, taking the item from me and holding it carefully. "Irritation looks good on you. Preston was that bad?"

"Actually, he was sort of nice. I'm just tired and had a rough time getting this."

She looks me over. "Yeah, you look like you got in a fight with a pile of dirt and lost. What's this about Preston being sort of nice?"

"He's been asking me out to be polite, and Claire was worried about me fitting in. He just wants to be friends."

She snorts. "Friends my ass."

"He also said Grey was a good guy, and he took the blame for the problems between them."

"Uh huh, sure, like the whole death problem?"

I shrug. "I'm not sure Preston did it."

She blows out a breath. "Maybe not. Or maybe like most sociopaths, he's good at pretending to be human." She holds up the cigar. "Thanks for this." She gives me a one-arm hug before heading back to her still running car. "I'll call you as soon as I know anything."

"Thanks for waiting up for me."

"Had to make sure you made it out alive."

Once I'm inside the house with the door locked, I unzip the side of my dress, letting out a breath of relief when my lungs have more room to breathe. "Thank the freaking gods."

"Thank God is right."

I scream and jump three feet in the air. "Grey! You scared the crap out of me."

He emerges from the darkened hallway and stalks toward me, stopping only inches away.

"Hi." His voice is rough. He doesn't touch me, his eyes taking in my dirty dress before returning to meet my eyes. "You're dirty."

A smile tugs at my lips at his innuendo, but it falters when I catch the heat in his gaze.

I'm already breathless from his sudden appearance. Throw in the stark appraisal, and warmth spreads low in my belly.

Just like that, the tension between us is so thick, it's a rope I could use to drag him to me.

"I should probably shower." My voice is low and hoarse.

He reaches for me then, a hand lifting toward my face.

My breath catches in my throat, waiting for what he's going to do.

He pulls a dead leaf out of my hair, lifting it in front of my face. "Showering might be a good idea."

I nod. We stare at each other, unmoving, unblinking. Wondering who's going to break first.

It's me. I break first.

"Grey." I reach for him, clearing the step between us and collide with his chest.

That's all it takes

His hands are in my hair, holding my head in place while his mouth crashes against mine.

I wrap my arms around him, pressing as close as possible while he devours me with his kiss.

We stand in the entryway, kissing, hands roaming until my lips are swollen and I've forgotten my own name.

"Shower with me," I say against lips.

He doesn't respond with words, instead lifting his shirt over his head. Immediately distracted by his leanly muscled frame, I trace my fingertips over his chest and down to his sweats, pushing them down.

He's already tugged down my dress, the fabric slumping around my waist. I help him, kicking off the heels and shoving the gown down to my feet, stepping out of the pile of clothes.

He moves back a pace, staring down at me, his gaze taking me in from head to toe. Just me in my strapless bra, panties, and thigh-high, sheer, black stockings.

He swallows and I track the movement.

I don't have a chance for insecurities to take root because he steps into me with a groan, tugging the cup of my bra down before dipping his head to take a nipple into his mouth.

"Grey." My legs sag, my hands reaching for his shoulders, but I needn't worry about falling because he lifts me into his arms bridal style.

"Time for that shower."

He races down the hall, dodging Bob as she meows

in irritation and skitters into the office, making us both laugh.

We're in the bathroom in seconds. He puts me down, turns the water on, then he's in front of me, removing off the rest of my clothes with a singular focus.

I can't assist him. I can't move. I can barely breathe. He takes off my bra, then my panties, leaving the stockings. I'm so turned on I can barely see straight. My whole body is sensitive, nerves on alert. Every brush of his fingers against my skin sends a live wire of electric need pulsing through me, simmering in my center.

Then Grey is kneeling in front of me on the bathmat, drawing down my stockings with slow, intentional movements.

"These are so sexy." His words are whispered, tickling against my inner thigh.

I gasp, one hand reaching behind me on the counter for support, the other sliding through his hair, luxuriating in the smooth strands tickling against my palm.

His mouth kisses a path down my legs as he removes first one stocking and then the next.

And then his head is between my legs and I squeak in surprise, leaning back against the sink, holding myself upright.

He spreads my thighs apart, widening my stance so he can run his tongue against me—so soft and yet so demanding.

While he tortures me with his mouth, the room fills

with steam and the wet sounds he's generating between my legs.

"Grey." His name is part plea, part whimper. Already he's learned exactly what I like, exactly how to push me over that edge.

And over the cliff I go, plunging into the depths of pleasure, the climax rushing over me, surrounding my entire body in wave after wave of sensation.

With one last faint kiss against my flesh, he stands and I slump against him.

He chuckles, pure satisfied male, and tightens his hold on me. "Now you're extra dirty."

"I might need help in the shower then," I speak into his chest.

"I can accommodate that."

I've already seen Grey naked in the living room the other night, but here, in the bathroom, lights ablaze and all at once, his body is nothing short of a revelation. He's all lean muscle, trim waist, strong legs and gorgeous man. And I get to feast on him.

In the shower, we get under the hot spray together, a tangle of wet limbs. I rinse off the dirt, and Grey washes my hair, turning the everyday task into a lesson in eroticism. Once I'm clean, my focus goes to my shower partner.

"I think you need extra soap." I lather my hands and then spread the slickness over his chest, aiming lower.

His hands brace on my shoulders as I work the soap lower and lower, gripping his length in my fingers and twisting my wrist as I work him up and down, reveling in the catch in his breath, the uncontrollable growl that breaks out of him.

"Jesus, Amelia."

Heat pools in me as I bask in his pleasure, reveling in his stomach muscles jumping and tightening under my hands, as I bring him to the brink. Knowing I can affect him as much as he affects me is a heady sensation.

He jerks in my palm, his fingers tightening on my shoulders. His face contorts and he moans as his orgasm rolls over him. He pulls me against him, holding me, catching his breath.

I get on my toes, stretching up to speak into his ear. "I want you inside me."

His arms clench around me. "I want that more than I want to breathe. But are you sure? If I don't make it through this—"

I pull back to meet his worried gaze. "I'm sure. I've never been more certain of anything in my life. I don't want to miss anything, not one minute, one moment of time with you. I want everything we can experience while we still can."

He nods, his eyes bright. "In that case, I may have left a present for you in the floorboards."

Giggling, movements clumsy in our haste, we get out of the shower and dry each other off. I race to the closet to open the secret compartment Grey showed me.

Back in my bedroom, Grey is stretched out on the bed in all his naked glory.

I hold up the condom package. "A hundred? That's ambitious."

He nods solemnly. "My goal is to use the whole box before I disappear again tonight."

I grimace and pace to the bed. "Sounds painful."

He laughs and tugs me down on top of him and there is nothing as glorious as spreading out on my bed and tangling with naked Grey, limbs twisting, mouths searching, exploring and playing with each other until we're both mad with desire.

I'm surrounded by a lust-fueled fog as Grey rolls on the condom and shifts between my thighs. I wrap my legs around him, staring up into his face while he pushes inside me, just an inch.

He gazes down at me, our eyes locked, then he thrusts again, another inch.

My hands run up his arms, tracing the rigid muscles and then clenching on his shoulders.

"Grey," my voice is a rough whisper of need.

Eyes still on mine, he drives in the final inches in one deep lunge and we both gasp at the rightness of the connection.

He blows out a breath and then his head dips, our foreheads touching. His mouth strokes against mine, a tender touch of flesh, and then we're kissing with abandon. I memorize the taste of his lips, the feel of his tongue against mine, the press of his hips. A crescendo of sensation.

He moves, driving into me in metered strokes,

advancing and retreating, layering pleasure atop pleasure, heat chasing over my skin and sensitizing every touch of his body against mine. My eyes shut and my head falls back, arching like a bow string begging to be plucked.

I open my eyes, meeting his gaze. He misses nothing, noting every catch of my breath and flutter of my eyes, his breath faltering every time my hands clench on his back or my legs flex.

Desire builds and builds. He moves faster, sensing the coming finale. He shifts closer, pushing his body exactly where I need it. That's all it takes for me to splinter into a thousand chords of bliss.

Grey shouts, shuddering, his arms tightening around me before he collapses, his weight pressing me into the mattress, the contrast of his hard body and the soft bedding making me sigh in contentment.

After a moment he rolls to the side, getting up to get rid of the condom before returning and drawing me into his arms.

"Do you need anything?" he asks, voice low.

I shake my head. "Just this," I murmur, snuggling further into his arms.

"I'm hungry."

I chuckle, the sound sleepy. "What else is new?"

"We haven't talked about what happened tonight with Preston."

"Oh, yeah." I push myself up on his chest. "Do you want to get food first, and then we can talk?"

He reaches up to push my hair back, then leans up to kiss me on the mouth. "Yes."

And then he disappears.

I gasp. He just winked out of existence. My heart lurches, then thunders in my chest.

No.

Blinking, I glance around the room as if he'll just magically reappear again right away.

"Dammit!" I slam my hands on the bed, eyes squeezing shut.

The bed sinks. "It's nice to see you so concerned about my departure."

My eyes fly open. I throw my arms around him as if that will keep him grounded in this time. "What the hell?"

"Yeah, that was not fun. Normally it's a little longer between moving there and back. That made me dizzy."

I must make some kind of noise because his voice softens, and he rubs my back. "It's okay. I'm here. If I go away, I'll come back."

I don't want to voice my fears, that one of these times he's going to vanish and never return.

"I'm going to get some food."

"I'm coming with you. I'll tell you about what happened tonight while you're cooking."

"Perfect."

I put on an oversized sleep shirt, and he grabs his sweats—which were still in the entryway on the floor—and then we migrate to the kitchen.

He makes grilled cheese sandwiches and I sit on the counter and relay everything that happened at the charity event, including what happened with Preston afterwards.

"So now we wait while Lexi's friend runs Don's DNA against mine." He brings the food over, setting a plate next to me on the counter before leaning over to brush a kiss against my shoulder. Then he stands next to me and picks up his own sandwich, taking a large bite.

We eat in contemplative silence. I should be thinking about what we're going to do to save Grey, but I'm too happy he's here. Too content. Too blissed out by his idle displays of affection. I don't want to go back to reality.

He devours his food like he always does, somehow consuming the whole thing before I can get even halfway through mine.

Wiping his hands on a napkin, he gets us both water and then resumes his position next to me, his hip pressing against my knee.

"I hope we can figure it out before it's too late."

A cold spear of dread pierces through my happy haze. We only have two weeks until Halloween. There's not enough time.

"We will. We have to."

He looks over at me, seeing straight through my bravado.

He steps in front of me, moving between my legs, his hands on either side of my hips. He kisses me on the forehead, then presses his lips to my temple, my cheek, then my mouth. "I will live. And then we will find each other."

I try to hang on to his words, hang on to *him*, hugging him against me like my arms can protect him from time itself.

But before I can respond, before I can kiss him again, my arms flop down, nothing substantial to hold them up anymore.

He's gone.

Chapter Twenty-One

"Don isn't Grey's father." Lexi sighs. "I feel like Maury Povich with all this baby-daddy nonsense. But they *are* related."

I press the phone closer to my ear like that will somehow make the meaning clearer. "What does that mean?" If Don isn't Grey's father, and Preston is his cousin . . . I can't wrap my head around it.

"Don is Grey's uncle. I had the lab compare Preston and Don too, since we had both samples, and Don is definitely Preston's father."

I sit in the recliner in the living room, gazing sightlessly out at the trees. Lexi wanted to meet for lunch, but I didn't want to leave the house, so I called her for the update. It's been a week since I last saw Grey. What if he shows up and I'm not here and I miss time with him? I don't want to miss even a minute.

"Which means if the paternity test attached to Joe's

trust affirms Grey as the heir and not Preston, Preston would have a real good reason to want Grey dead."

"Who stands to lose the most?" I ask.

Lexi's response is automatic. "Preston, for sure."

"Who else?"

"Not anyone worth thinking about."

"We have to look at all angles, you have to agree with that. So. Who else stands to lose the most if this information gets out? No matter how unlikely."

She releases a heavy exhale. "Claire? I mean, I honestly can't believe it, but I also wouldn't believe she could sleep with Don. It's so gross. But I don't think it's possible."

"Are we sure?"

"She works the festival every year on Halloween. There would have been many, many witnesses to verify her alibi. Besides she's too frail to push Grey down the steps or bash his head in."

I drum my fingers on the armrest of the recliner. "Maybe she hired someone."

"Maybe. She always acted like Grey was like a son to her. Her and Bonnie were good friends."

"Were they though? If Bonnie was sleeping with Joe and Claire was sleeping with Don?"

Lexi pauses for a second to consider. "Okay, so she has motive, but she doesn't have the strength and didn't have the time. I don't think it's her."

My eyes fall shut and I consider everything. We're running out of time. Halloween is in one week. What if we're too late? He'll be on guard, sure, but is it enough? I've tried to go back to his time, and I can't. I won't be able to save him.

What if he doesn't come back? What if this last time was *the* last time? It can't be. He's coming back.

But what if he doesn't? The thought is a lead weight in my belly, ready to drag me down.

"Let's go out for dinner and talk about it," says Lexi.

"I can't . . . I have work to do."

"Work?"

"I'm under a deadline." Ha. My deadline is next month. I haven't written a single thing and there's no way I'm going to. I mean, it's kind of a lie but it's a true lie.

"Ugh, fine. You're acting just like Grey did."

"I am?"

"Yes. We used to go out for dinner every Friday night but before he died, he kept flaking on me with random excuses. He never wanted to leave the house and he was always wearing this ridiculous pink and purple robe—he was really acting off at the end there. There must have been something I'm still missing."

Bob races around the living room and zooms down the hall. "I gotta go. Call me if you hear anything else."

"Will do."

We hang up and I follow Bob down the hall. Maybe she's racing around because Grey is back.

But that hope is dashed. The rooms are empty and silent.

On a whim, I go to the closet and pull up the loose board in the corner.

My heart leaps. There's a piece of paper tucked inside with a box underneath it.

I miss you.

I press it to my chest. "I miss you, too," I whisper.

I open the small box. More condoms. I laugh and tears fill my eyes.

Great. Prophylactics are making me cry.

Knock, knock, knock.

I turn off the light and head to the front door.

"Claire." She's standing on my porch, elegant in soft brown pants and a creamy blouse. Her cane today is sturdy and dark, the wood shiny, the handle a smooth ivory. In her free hand, she's holding a pastry box.

"Amelia, I brought you some pie."

"Oh, you shouldn't have." I take the container. "Thank you so much." I peer behind her to see if Preston is waiting, but there's no black BMW, just a sporty gold Mercedes. "Would you like to come in?"

Bob hisses from the hallway, back arched.

"Oh," Claire laughs nervously. "Who is this?"

"Bob. Sorry, she attacks people. Let me put her in the bedroom." I pick up Bob under one arm, the pie in the other, and then call over my shoulder. "Come on in. Make yourself at home."

I put Bob in my bedroom and then head back to the kitchen.

Claire takes a seat at the dining table, gazing out the

window, shoulders straight, posture perfect enough to balance an apple on her head.

It's hard to imagine her sleeping with Don. Why did she do it? Was it just one night of drunken passion? Did Joe know?

Does any of it matter?

"Would you like some tea?" I place the pie box on the counter.

"Yes, please."

I turn the kettle on, reaching into the cupboard to grab a couple of mugs. "Earl Grey all right?"

"Do you have anything without caffeine?"

"I have some honey lavender. How does that sound?"

"Perfect."

While the kettle is heating, I open the pie box to take a whiff. "This smells amazing."

"It's apple pie. Not as good as the strawberry rhubarb, but I'm making a big batch in a few days for the upcoming Halloween faire."

"I've heard you volunteer there every year." The kettle clicks off and I pour the steaming water into our cups.

"I do." She nods, smiling at me, but then the smile droops. "This year I won't be able to make it, but I am making extra pies for the children."

"Do you have other plans?" I bring the mugs out, sitting across from her at the table.

"No. It's just my arthritis, you see. It's getting harder

every year and when the weather starts turning, every-thing aches more."

"I'm sorry," I murmur, blowing on the steaming tea.

"It's fine, dear." She reaches over, setting her frail hand over mine for a brief moment. "I'll make sure to bring you some of the strawberry rhubarb next weekend."

"You don't have to trouble yourself."

She waves a hand at me. "It's no trouble. I've been meaning to stop by to talk to you about your grandparents. They were such dear people. Your grandfather was incredibly generous with the church and all of our local causes."

"Did you know them well?" I take a small sip of the hot tea.

"We moved in different circles. Your grandparents were a bit older than me. They had a wonderful love story."

Claire shares what she knows, how my grandparents met and got married right after high school, how my grandfather worked in a factory owned by Blake Indus-tries and worked his way up from laborer to head mechanic.

"Your grandparents had a hard time conceiving. Did you know that?"

I shake my head.

"We had that in common, your grandmother Cecelia and I. They had your father quite young and then were unable to bear any more children. I married Joseph when

I was twenty-two and I was over forty when Preston was finally born."

"Wow."

She chuckles. "It's hard to believe my miracle baby is thirty now. They told us we wouldn't be able to have children, you know."

I have no idea how to respond to this. Was this why she cheated? Because she wanted to bear a son so badly? Joe couldn't have been impotent, not if Bonnie was able to conceive Grey a few years later.

"I've never been in this cabin before. It's very quaint."

I startle at the subject change. "Thank you. I am enjoying it very much. It's quiet."

"You haven't had any other problems or troubles since your first night here?"

"Nope. No troubles at all."

She smiles. "That's wonderful. I should be going. Thank you for the tea, it was lovely."

I'm not sure she so much as touched the tea, but I nod anyway.

"I have to meet Preston at home, and he'll worry if I'm late." She uses her cane to push herself to standing, and I get up from my chair.

"I'll walk you out." I open the front door. "Do you need help to your car?" I ask, eyeballing my sagging porch and wondering if I have liability insurance.

"It's fine, dear, thank you. I'll see you soon."

I watch her make her way, one slow shuffle step at a

time, bearing her weight on her cane. Once she's safely in her car and has disappeared down the drive, I release a breath and shut the door.

Meoooow. Bob protests her confinement. I let her out before heading back to the kitchen to clean up.

It was nice of Claire to bring me the pie, to stop by and spend some time telling me stories about my grandparents.

My mind spins around the things she told me, and what I know about her marriage to Joe, her relationship with Don. It does seem unbelievable that she could be a murderer, but she might have even more of a reason than Preston to not want the knowledge of his paternity to get out.

I finish with the dishes and stare out the back window at the towering evergreens, wishing Grey would reappear, wishing we had more time. But we don't. Even now, the clock ticks, time marching unrelentingly toward Grey's death.

Fear slithers through me.

What if we can't stop it? What if this is all I get, this one little crack in time? What if I never see Grey again, and even worse, what if like my father and Constance, I forget all about him?

Before I can spiral into complete and utter depression, a thump echoes from the front of the house.

I race in that direction. Maybe it's him.

"Grey?"

The second I open the door, a series of taps rattles across the front steps of the porch.

What was that? I glance around, but the front yard is empty and still. I step forward, gaze down.

It's pebbles. Someone threw a palm-sized, open bag full of pebbles onto my porch. What the hell?

My head whips back. A heavy object thumps onto the patio at my feet.

It's a rock. I've been hit in the head with a rock. Shocked, the assault doesn't quite register until pain blooms on the side of my head.

Heart pounding, I step back, ready to flee back inside but stop when something moves near the trees up front, about a hundred yards away.

It's a tall figure in a black cloak and mask. He's holding a knife. A big knife, like a machete.

Stumbling backward, I press a hand to my head— and run into something warm, surprise yanking a shriek from my throat.

Chapter Twenty-Two

"It's me." His hands grip my shoulders from behind.

Grey.

The relief is so sudden and so complete it leaves me lightheaded. I slump back against him.

"Are you okay?"

Numbly I point at the figure down in the driveway.

Grey stiffens, then rumbles behind me.

Is he actually growling?

Before I can turn around and check, he's released my shoulders and racing down the porch straight for the knife-wielding maniac.

What the hell is he doing?

The figure remains motionless for just a split second, then they sprint away, down the gravel drive and out of sight.

Distantly, a car engine turns over, a door slams, the revving moving away from the house.

Grey stops, just before the hill curves downward, his hands on his hips, staring in the direction the figure disappeared.

He shakes his head, then turns and jogs back to the porch.

"What was that all about?" he asks.

"I don't know. Kids playing pranks?"

He kicks the heavy rock on my porch away and then reaches for me, one hand cupping my cheek, the other hovering over where the rock struck me. Frown lines etch his mouth, grooves settling between his brows. "You're hurt. Let's go inside and I'll clean you up."

In the bathroom, he sits me on the sink and carefully cleans my wound. It's really nothing, just a bruise and a small scratch, but Grey's face is a picture of concern for me and anger for . . . whoever the knife-wielding maniac was.

"I could have killed that bastard." His jaw clenches as he finishes patting the side of my head dry and then tosses the antiseptic wipe into the trash.

"I'm sure it was just a prank gone awry. Maybe they didn't mean to hit me. Probably just trying to scare me. We have something more concerning to worry about."

"What? My imminent death?"

"No, the fact that they probably saw you."

Confusion clouds his eyes for a second and then his expression turns sheepish. "Oh, yeah. They think I'm dead." He chuckles.

"This isn't funny. People already hate me because

they think I'm some demon witch, and now they're going to think I've conjured you."

He smirks. "You kind of have. If by conjure you mean you've cast a spell and charmed me into your heart. One might say, it's a total eclipse of the heart."

"That doesn't even make sense." I smack him on the arm and laugh.

He shrugs and kisses me, a quick brush of his lips. "If anyone asks, I'm haunting you, okay? It's not your fault. I've taken control, just like Janet Jackson." He leans in again and kisses my neck and I sigh and wrap my arms around him. "Besides, the mind has a way of making logic from the illogical. I'm sure they'll come up with a perfectly rational explanation for seeing someone who resembles me on your property. Maybe they'll think I'm Preston. They were far enough away, and they had some kind of ski mask on, obscuring their view. I'm sure it will be fine."

I sigh. He's probably right. "Okay."

"Okay? It's that easy?"

"It is if you keep kissing me like that. It's been too long."

"Agreed."

We get lost in each other, kissing, touching, savoring every sensation for a few long minutes before reality intrudes, wedging into my thoughts.

There are things I have to tell him.

I pull away, blinking to clear the lust fog from my mind. "Don isn't your father."

He blows out a breath. "Thank the time lords for that."

"He's Preston's father."

He winces. "Poor bastard. So, then we know for sure that Joe is my dad?"

I bite my lip. "Barring some secret Blake brother no one knows about, yes. I think I have other things to tell you, too."

"Okay." He glances around. "Maybe we should leave the bathroom."

"Good idea."

He steps back and I hop off the sink.

"Do you want some pie?" I ask while we're walking to the kitchen. "Claire brought some by earlier."

"Hell yeah."

We eat and I tell him everything Lexi said, plus everything Claire revealed during her visit.

"I asked Claire what she thought about my mom's death," he says when I'm done.

"What did she say?"

He opens his mouth and then winks out of existence.

Before I can even register that he's left, still blinking at the chair where he was sitting just a second ago, he reappears in the same spot.

His eyes widen. "Whoa."

I swallow. "That was weird. Sort of like what happened before, except faster."

He nods. "I don't know what's going on."

We take a moment, waiting to see if he's going to stick this time, and when he doesn't vanish into thin air, he continues our conversation where we left off.

"Claire told me—" He rubs the back of his neck, "She said my mom was seeing a psychiatrist before she passed. She had been having some issues with depression." He shakes his head. "I had no idea."

I move into him, crawling into his lap and hugging him tight. "It wasn't your fault."

His arms wrap around me. "I know. I can't change any of it, any more than you can change what happened with your parents. Which was also not your fault, Amelia."

I take a deep breath. I wish I could believe those words. I wish I could take them inside and make them true, but I can't. Maybe I didn't cause their death, but I chose to let them believe I hated them. I could have called them, could have said something, could have forgiven them. But I didn't. No wonder the magic closet doesn't work for me. I'm broken. "Why is everything so hard?"

His words are gentle puffs of air against my skin. "My mom used to say your heart will shatter a thousand times over in life, but in the end, it will make the most beautiful collage."

I lean back, meeting his misty gaze. "That's amazing."

He nods. "She was amazing."

We hold each other for a few minutes before I get

out of his lap and stand to put away the pie, what's left of it. It's three-quarters gone and I only had one slice. Grey can eat like no one I've ever met.

"Well." He leans back in the chair, stretching his arms up over his head. His shirt pulls up and I take a second to ogle while he keeps speaking. "It's almost D-day and we are no closer to figuring this out than we were before. What if it's something completely off the wall we haven't considered?"

My eyes flick up to his. "Like what?"

He grins at my blatant gawking. "What if it wasn't anything related to the Blakes and Joe's will? What if it was an accident? Maybe some random stranger broke into my house to . . . steal my *Princess Bride* first edition VHS?"

I smother a laugh. "As much as that VHS might be worth, I'm not sure that's a strong enough motivation for murder."

His eyes glitter up at me. "We'll figure it out. Together. Because I just found you, and I won't lose you."

I nod. Resolute. "We need to come up with some kind of plan for Halloween."

Thirty minutes later, we're snuggling on the couch and no closer to figuring out how to stop Grey from dying. Also, Grey has disappeared and reappeared twice more.

"What if I leave? What if I just go somewhere else?"

"Maybe. But what if you just die at a later date, and I can't help you? What if your killer just does it somewhere else?"

"Yeah, I don't like the idea of running or kicking the can down the road." His arm is wrapped around me, his fingers rubbing my back. "I need to face this head on, resolve it now. If I disappear and learn anything of significance, I'll put a note in the closet."

I nod against his chest. "Okay."

"We should consider also what will happen if we succeed. If this works. If I don't die and the past changes."

I pull back to meet his eyes. "We might forget. Like my dad did . . . until he found the obituary. I wonder if Constance remembered anything."

He shrugs. "No real way of knowing."

Our eyes lock.

I press my lips together in thought. "We should put stuff in the closet. The original obituary survived the change in there."

He nods. "I have an idea."

A few minutes later, we're in the closet and he's grabbed his old Polaroid camera from the living room. I dusted it off but left it on the shelves along with the DeLorean and golden head statue, which Grey told me is some collectible from *Indiana Jones*.

"Is that thing going to work?"

He examines the clunky black camera in his hand. "It

has a few more films left. I bet it will. They knew how to build things back then, but I guess we'll find out."

He holds it out in front of us and snaps a shot while kissing my cheek. The camera clicks and buzzes as the photograph emerges. He pulls it out and sets it on the floor in a shadow to develop.

He takes another shot, both of us smiling this time.

"Silly faces now, go." He snaps the button.

We review the pictures together, laughing at each other's expressions, and then stick them in the secret compartment.

Grey shakes a few condoms out of the box and throws them on top of the photos. "Because if we do get reunited, we'll need these."

"*When* we get reunited," I correct him.

Our eyes lock. He smiles. "When we get reunited." He leans in to kiss me. "When," he whispers against my lips.

The kiss flows from sweet to scorching in seconds.

I pick up one of the condoms from the floor. "Maybe we should use one of these while we're in here."

"Yes," he breathes, already tugging my shirt over my head, careful of the bruise on my head.

<hr>

A few orgasms later, we're stretched out, facing each other, not speaking, just touching, letting our bodies cool and waiting as time rolls inexorably forward.

"Where were you three years ago?" His thumb brushes my cheek.

I wiggle into him, moving my leg over his hip to get closer. "That was six months after my parents died and I was . . . not in the best place. I was only a month or two away from publishing that damn article." I tilt my head. "Maybe you could stop me from hitting publish."

He smiles, but it doesn't quite reach his eyes. "Maybe I—"

Before he can finish the sentence, he's gone.

Chapter Twenty-Three

Halloween arrives, the day brisk and chilly, but bright and sunny. Clear blue skies as far as the eye can see. It's horrible.

The outside world might be beautiful, but inside, I'm falling apart and there's absolutely nothing I can do about anything. It's been a week since Grey was last here and now, we're out of time.

I have zero control over what's happening to Grey three years ago, just like I couldn't stop my parents' deaths. Just like I couldn't go back in time and tell them I love them and don't hate them. At least Grey knows how I feel about him . . . except I didn't tell him I loved him, either. He knows, though. He has to know. What if he doesn't know?

I have enough regrets from my parents' death, I don't need any more. I'm so stuffed with guilt, it's leaking out of my pores.

How do you let go when you wish you could change so many things?

But I know the answer is to release control. I can't go back to Grey's time any more than I can go back to my parents' time. I can't change the choices I've already made, I can only pledge to do better going forward.

I stand on the back porch and whisper into the wind. "I'm sorry. I promise from here on to honor your memories. If time moves forward, even if Grey isn't here, I can change my story. I can tell the real story. I might let Colleen down, I might lose everything for breach of contract or whatever. But I can live my truth. No more regrets."

I pace the house, checking the closet compartment every five minutes until I need to do something else or I might go out of my mind. I've barely seen Bob all day, she's been hiding under the bed like she's depressed Grey is gone, too.

Evening approaches, which means the seconds are ticking ever closer to what will be the end, or maybe a new beginning.

Please, let it be the latter.

A tapping at the front door makes me nearly leap out of my skin.

Jittery, I race to open it.

"Claire." She's wearing soft gray slacks and a dark gray blouse. It's as casual as I've ever seen her. Her cane today is dark and shiny, black as night, gemstones glittering at the top. She's holding a pie.

Oh, right. She said she would be bringing the straw-berry rhubarb.

"Amelia. I hope I'm not disturbing you." She peers behind me into the house.

"No. Please come in." I step back, a mixture of emotions twisting through me. I'm grateful to have some kind of distraction, something else to think about, but I also want her to leave. I don't want to invite her in. What if Grey reappears? What if he needs me?

Claire takes the same seat at the dining table she used before, and I make some tea.

I slice the pie and make up plates for both of us while Claire describes the happenings at the festival, how adorable the children were in their costumes, and all the fun games and rides they had set up.

"Are you planning on going down to the fairgrounds tonight?" she asks me, blowing on her tea.

"What? No. Uh, maybe next year." I take a bite of the pie.

"Do you like it?"

"It's delicious," I lie. I can't taste anything, nerves making everything taste like sawdust in my mouth.

She smiles serenely. "Maybe by next year people will have warmed up and you won't have to worry about making an appearance."

I nod. "Yes. Totally." What is she talking about? Oh, she's assuming I'm avoiding the festival because people hate me. If only it was just that.

She sets her cane against the table, the curve of the

handle facing me. It's carved into some kind of wolf head or something. Interesting.

"Next year, we're planning on having a Ferris wheel at the festival. I think the children will love it." She watches me take another bite and self-consciousness brushes over me.

Maybe she'll actually drink her tea this time. Or eat her own slice of pie. It's still sitting in front of her, uneaten, fork untouched.

"That sounds amazing." My eyes sweep over her untouched food, and then stop on the cane at her side and stick.

I can't look away. There's something familiar about the wolf, it's eyes. Maybe she's used this cane before.

I blink. The eyes are gemstones. Bloodred gemstones. Marquise shaped. At least three carats. My heart stops then resumes beating, pounding in my chest. The skin covering my entire body flashes hot and then cold.

Oh, shit. My throat is closing up. My mind races. I can't let her know.

I put my fork down, the silverware clattering onto the table. I clear my throat and wonder if I can take a sip of my tea without my hands shaking and sloshing it all over myself.

"Your cane." I manage the words without trembling. "It's really neat." If I sound off or strange, she doesn't let on.

Her smile is luminous. "Joseph had this made for me

many years ago. The eyes are red diamonds, did you know?"

I shake my head.

"They're rare. Expensive. I lost one of the stones, years ago. It was quite the ordeal to have another setting placed. I didn't realize until then how much Joe had spent on me, how much he had cared. He did care for me, despite some of our history, you know."

I nod, numb with shock. My ears are ringing. This can't be right.

Claire was here in this house.

She said the other day she'd never been here. That was a lie.

My mind is buzzing. She had an alibi. That's why we dismissed her as a suspect. If she was at the festival all night, how could she have done it? There's no way she could have driven here, killed Grey, and then gone back. Someone would have noticed. It would have taken too long.

My thoughts in a jumble, I move my gaze down to the half-eaten pie in front of me.

Ice-cold terror slices through me.

What if something is in this pie? The last one was fine but . . . I don't like the way she's staring at me. Calculating. Waiting. What if she was able to drug Grey and kill him after the fair because he was passed out from . . . *oh my God.*

"Preston was a miracle baby. Did you know that?"

I swallow. I need water. I need to purge this pie out of my system. I need to run. Hide. Warn Grey. But how?

What is she talking about? Preston?

"What?" I can't feel my hands. Is it shock or poison?

"Joe couldn't have kids. Well, it was unlikely he could have kids, that's how the doctor said it." She rolls her eyes and huffs out an irritated laugh.

My mouth pops open. She's all but admitting Preston isn't Joe's son. He's Don's. She really did sleep with Don.

Oh God, that means . . . Preston wasn't the miracle baby. Grey was.

She rubs her lips together and sighs. "Bonnie gave Joe something I could not." Her eyes are bleak. But then they harden. "She had something I could never have. Could never buy. He was going to leave me for her. After almost fifty years, he was going to choose her over me." She shakes her head sadly. "I gave him the best years of my life, and he wanted to throw it all away. He didn't appreciate anything I did for him. That's why she had to go."

I manage to unstick my tongue from the roof of my mouth to ask, "Why are you telling me this?"

"Bonnie loved this pie." She nods down at the table and smiles.

This is so creepy. It's like she can't even hear me.

"Grey did as well."

No. The sound of his name releases me from the

frozen panic clutching me in its grip. I lurch up, out of the chair. I need to get this pie out of me.

But Claire moves faster than what should be possible. Using her cane, she trips me. I slam into the floor, knocking my head against the linoleum.

The impact makes me grunt, my head throbbing. I try to catch my breath while she pushes herself up to standing.

I can't get up, but I can do something. From the floor, I stick my fingers down my throat and gag.

"Oh, sweetie. It's too late for that."

"You're not going to get away with this," I heave, sounding like the worst heroine in every damn horror movie.

I have to stop this. I have to warn Grey. Despair swamps me. I've never been able to get through the damn portal. What makes it different now?

"I already have gotten away with this. Many times. It's just a matter of time for the drugs to kick in."

I moan, unable to fight the rising tide of panic. My stomach churns.

Grey. He won't think anything of eating Claire's pie, considering we just ate some together the other night. Even now, he could be in his time being poisoned. I have to get to the closet. I have to get back to him.

She crouches down next to me, gripping her cane in one hand. "Don't worry. It's just a sleeping pill. Can't put anything in your system that might show up in a tox screen if they ever find you. You'll go to sleep and then you'll just disappear." She reaches out her free hand and brushes some hair off of my face, her hand soft and tender. "And no one will care. No one will know. You have no family. No real friends. No one in this town likes you anyway. Don't worry so much, darling."

"Why are you doing this?"

"Why am I doing this?" She pushes herself to standing, glaring down at me. "You brought this on yourself. It's unfortunate you've been talking about Grey, making people curious. I tried to warn you. I tried to scare you out of town, but you just wouldn't leave."

What? Is she behind the pranks, the cloaked figure with a knife? That wasn't Claire. They were too large. There's no way she could run like they did.

"Did you kill Grey because he was Joe's son?"

Her face hardens. "He was going to give his bastard son and that whore everything. Everything. He wanted a divorce. He wanted to be with her. I couldn't let that happen. So, I made sure it didn't."

Holy shit, did she kill Bonnie, too?"

She keeps ranting. "Everything was fine for nearly three years. But then he was going to leave me again. I couldn't let that happen. Think of the scandal. I couldn't let him do that to Preston. After everything I sacrificed for him. He told me he was going to leave me, change his will, but I didn't realize he already had." She thumps the cane against the floor. "Grey was asking too many questions about his mother's death. There were too many loose ends. He had to go."

I try to figure out what she's saying. It's like we're having two separate conversations here. And then it clicks. She killed Grey and Bonnie, and she killed Joe, too.

Holy hell.

"Joe had a stroke." The words wheeze out.

"Joe loved my pie, too." She smiles.

She gave him something to induce the stroke. He already had health issues. It was probably easy. She volunteers at the hospital holding babies.

Nausea rolls through me.

I have so many questions. I need to keep her talking before I fall asleep. My eyes are getting heavy, fog filling my brain. "How did you kill Grey? You couldn't have been here. You were at the festival all night."

She smiles down at me. "That's my little secret. Are you getting tired yet? Just a few more minutes and everything will be over. You won't feel a thing. I'm not a monster." She glances over at the clock, her gaze averted.

Now.

Mustering every ounce of strength and will in my body, I push myself up and race for the closet.

"Amelia," Claire calls out from behind me. "You won't get far."

She probably thinks I'm running outside. Good. I open the front door, letting it slam against the wall, and then as quickly as I can, I sprint down the hall.

I waste precious seconds shutting the bedroom door

behind me as quietly as I can, and then the same with the closet door.

The drugs are definitely kicking in. Grogginess fills my head, my movements are slow like I'm moving through water, but I'm still moving. I'm not dead yet. And neither is Grey. I can't accept that.

I pull up the board in the closet. There's nothing there. Is it too late?

I sit on the floor in the back of the closet, keeping my eyes open—I can't close them, I'll fall asleep. I stare at the door and breathe in and out.

It's not long before Claire's figured out my ruse. The door in the bedroom clicks open.

Claire's cane clomps on the hardwood, getting closer.

A wave of dizziness crashes over me. No.

I put all my energy into thinking about Grey. About how he's meant to be mine, and I'm meant to be his. About how I won't give up. How he's worth every last minute I have left, and I'm worth it, too.

I blink and barely hold in my gasp. The light is off. The closet door is wide open. My clothes are gone, and hanging in their place are men's shirts, jackets. Boots and sneakers are scattered around me on the floor.

Holy shit.

It worked.

My first instinct is to yell, scream, race out of the closet and find Grey, but what if she's here now, in this time?

I have to be careful.

I stand up and the world tilts around me. Stumbling through the doorway, I fall into the bed.

So much for being quiet.

But there's no responding noise. No crash or shuffle step of Claire with her cane.

Holding onto the wall, I wade through the house, somehow making it into the kitchen, coming to a breathless halt.

Grey.

He's here. Slumped over the dining table. The pie in front of him a quarter gone.

No. I stumble over to him, collapsing beside him.

No, no, no, he ate too much, too quickly. As usual.

"Please don't be dead," the words are whispered, a prayer. I push at his shoulder. His head lolls to one side and I press my fingers against his neck, trying to feel for a pulse. I'm breathing too fast, my fingers shaking, my own heart thundering in my ears, but I finally feel his pulse, fluttering against my finger.

It's there. I lean over, resting my head next to his. He's breathing. His breaths are low and shallow. He needs medical attention. We need to call someone, the phone, we need . . . Wait a minute.

Where's Claire?

My eyes droop. They're fitted with weights. I need to sleep, just for a minute.

I shake my head. Can't.

This is insane. Impossible. How are we going to get

out of this when I'm drugged, Grey is drugged, he can't even move, it's too late!

I can't drag his heavy ass to the closet.

Maybe I can bring us both back, but wait. No. Claire is there, in my time.

I shake my head like it will clear the fog from my thoughts.

Hopelessness smothers me. We're going to die. Both of us.

So mired in turmoil, I almost miss the thump of someone pounding up the patio steps. The front door bangs open. Footsteps approach.

It's not like Claire's cane shuffle. These are sturdy and sure.

I lift up my impossibly heavy head toward the sound.

Don steps into view. "Who the hell are you?"

"What are you doing here?" My words are slurred and I almost laugh. I sound hammered.

His face clouds in anger and he stomps toward us.

Oh, hell.

I cower over Grey, a feeble attempt to protect him.

Something tugs in my stomach, I think I'm going to be sick, but then I collapse on the floor, on top of Grey.

I blink and my eyes dart around.

Don is gone. I'm sprawled on the floor with Grey, still in the dining room.

Wait. This is my time. We both moved through the portal together.

"Where are you?" Claire shrieks. She's still back in

the bedroom area, searching for me, but it's only a matter of time before she comes in here.

I can't believe we traveled together. I wasn't even trying that time. The portal must be pushing us on its own. Do I have any control?

"Grey. Wake up." I lift up and smack him on the cheek, but he's out. He's bigger than me, but he also ate a lot more.

The shuffle step of Claire with her cane gets louder.

She's coming this way.

Frantically, I search for some sort of weapon.

No, wait. The phone. I can call 9-1-1.

I glance up toward the wall, then down at Grey. I don't want to leave Grey unprotected, but I don't have a choice. Pushing myself to standing, I shuffle toward the landline. My legs are like jelly, wobbling underneath me.

I lean heavily against the counter and yank the phone off the wall and dial.

A gasp has me spinning around.

Claire stares down at Grey, her face pale as a ghost. "This is impossible."

Then her eyes narrow and she picks up her cane, pulling it up and behind her head.

Fear stabs through my heart.

That's how she killed him.

"No!" Abandoning the phone, I throw myself over Grey.

I wait for the thud of the cane against my back, my head, but it never comes. Someone is talking, a man.

I lift my head from Grey's back and glance around. My breath escapes in short, quiet gasps.

Back again to Grey's time. Don is here in the kitchen, his back to us. He's on the phone talking to someone.

"Some woman was here with him."

I try to calm my breathing. He didn't hear us. I'm holding my breath. Barely breathing. If he turns around . . .

"No, I don't know who it was. I can't take care of him. They both vanished."

Grey chooses that opportune moment to snore loudly.

Don spins around.

Blink.

We're back with Claire.

I think I have to throw up now.

She's staring at us, still standing in the dining room where she was moments before, eyes wide with shock.

I need something to defend us. We can't just keep going back and forth between two deranged killers.

Claire shuffles closer, clutching her cane in both of her hands. What is she going to do? Bash us both with it?

Her eyes are wild, mouth arranged in a snarl.

Yep. That's exactly what she's going to do.

Yeeooowwwwll!

A flying orange tabby leaps off the back of the

couch, latching on to Claire's arm, a bundle of claws and teeth and growls.

Claire screams, waving her hands wildly. Bob goes flying, slamming against the counter and with a thump, she goes still.

My heart shatters. Horror, denial, and pain thunder through me, shaking me from my stupor.

But Bob may have just saved us. Claire doesn't have a good grip on the cane anymore. I leap up and grab for it. She has it around the center, but I have the top, near the head. We struggle for it. She's stronger than she appears, or the drugs have made me weaker than I realized, but with a hard yank, it slips from her grasp.

I'm not expecting it. Stumbling backwards, I nearly fall over Grey.

The world morphs around us.

Don is right in front of me. Drawing on every last reserve of strength left in my body, I swing the cane and it *thwaps* the side of his head, the impact jarring up my arms into my shoulders.

There's a flash of bright light, then total, utter blackness.

Chapter Twenty-Four

"Amelia? What happened?"

We're not in bed this time, more's the pity.

We're not really anywhere. The space is empty. I'm surrounded by hazy, gray mist.

"Grey? Where are you?" I can't see him, just the fog.

My body is heavy and weighted, like it normally is in the in-between, but my mind is clear.

I reach into the mist and he's there, his hand sliding up my arm to my neck, tugging me into him. I wrap my arms around his steady presence, my cheek against his chest.

"We did it," I murmur into him.

"You did it." His voice rumbles through me.

"Me and Bob." I gasp. "Bob."

His arms tighten. "She'll be okay. We'll all be okay."

"What happens now?" I ask.

"I don't know."

I swallow through the emotion rising up my throat. "Don't forget me."

"Don't you forget about me."

My laughter is wet. "Seriously?"

He chuckles. "I could never forget you, you know, no matter what happens."

I grip him tighter. "If everything works out, you'll go back to your time and you won't meet me for another three years."

"I've been thinking about that, and maybe not."

"What do you mean?"

Awareness is receding. The grey mist is coalescing around us, tugging us apart.

"Wait for me!"

Chapter Twenty-Five

December 2012

"What if he hates me? What if he regrets his offer and kicks me out?" I glance over at Bob, lounging in the passenger seat, yawning.

I sigh. "You should really show more concern. We could both end up homeless wretches."

She stares at me like I'm an idiot.

"You're right. It's fine. It will all be fine. We're almost there."

My palms are slick with nerves. I put on my blinker and turn up the gravel drive toward the cabin.

I can't believe I have family. After my parents died six months ago, I thought I had no living relatives. Then out of nowhere, I get a call from my dad's dad. A grandfather. I have a grandfather. Sure, it's just him and me, but that's better than just me and me.

My breath catches in my throat when I pull up to the cabin. It's exactly how I pictured it based on his description.

Quaint and cozy, nestled amongst the towering pines. It's been recently painted, the white paint and blue trim glowing against the backdrop of green.

"We're here, Bob." I pull the carrier out of the back, and she hops into it. She must be as anxious as I am to get out of the truck.

Heart thumping, Bob and I make our way up the porch, and I knock.

"Amelia."

My grandfather looks exactly like Dad if he had lived longer. Same warm eyes, wide mouth, strong nose, just weathered with age. His hair is longish and pulled back, the grey and white strands tugged away from his face.

I have to blink back the emotion rising in my eyes. I clear my throat and pull myself together. "Mr. Peters?" I wasn't sure what to call him. Grandpa or Poppa might be pushing it since we've never met. This is so surreal, but oh so exciting.

"Please come in, come in." He takes my hand, his grasp like warm, softened leather.

He leads me down the narrow entry, through a living room that opens on one side into a kitchen and dining area. There is a tray of food laid out on the table, along with a tea service.

I blink at the tray of meat and cheese and snacks laid out, along with my favorite brand of tea.

Huh. How did he know what I like? Maybe he likes the same things.

"Who's this?" He peers into the crate.

"This is Bob. She's the cat I told you about." When he called and asked me to live in the family cabin, I told him I had a pet just in case that was a deal breaker.

"You can let her out if you like. This is her place now, too."

"She can be a little . . . violent around men."

He chuckles, the sound raspy and deep. "That's a useful trait. I'm sure she'll be fine. She'll have to get used to me."

My heart swells and I nod. "All right, I'll just let her out over here." I step into the living room and put the crate on the couch before I open it, giving Bob my best "be good" glare before opening her door.

She hops out, sniffs the air delicately, then bolts toward the entry before disappearing down a hallway.

"I enjoy cats. They're independent creatures. We could never have one because your grandmother was allergic." He clears his throat and then gestures to the table. "Would you like some food?"

"Yes, please. This is my favorite tea, did you know?"

We sit at the table and he hands me a napkin, shaking his head. "I didn't. This was all put together by my last renter. He's been helping me fix this place up for your arrival."

"Wow. That's really nice of him."

He nods. "He's a good man. He's been through some rough times. We've had quite an interesting couple months here in Mystic Falls."

"The town is gorgeous. The drive through downtown was amazing." I put some cheese and grapes from the tray onto a plate and then stare at the setting. Déjà vu flows through me. Something about this is all so familiar.

"It's a lovely place to live. You're going to enjoy it. I'm very happy that you came, and that you're here."

"Thank you for calling me. I never would have known you existed. Dad never," I shake my head, "he never said anything."

He takes a sip of tea and then meets my gaze. "I'm sorry I didn't reach out to him sooner."

I swallow through a rising lump in my throat. "I—I know. I feel the same way." I avert my eyes. I can't tell him everything, not yet. But he's not the only one with guilt. I didn't reach out either, even when I should and now it's too late.

But it's not too late to connect with each other now, and here.

We eat and drink tea as he talks about the town, where to get groceries, the best places to eat, and the upcoming holiday festivities.

After we eat, he shows me around and helps me grab my suitcase and other meager possessions from the back of the truck.

We've only grabbed a few boxes and we're heading

back for more when the crunch of gravel has us both pausing. A dark blue Porsche SUV stops behind my faded old truck, and a petite woman with dark curly hair slips out of the driver's side door.

She waves as she approaches, a manila folder in one hand. "Hey, Mr. Peters." She sticks her hand in my direction when she reaches us. "You must be Amelia. I've heard so much about you."

Her handshake is firm and swift, and a surge of déjà vu rolls over me. Have I met her before?

Mr. Peters nods in greeting. "This is Lexi Stone. She's a local attorney who's helping us with the paperwork for the property."

"It's nice to meet you."

Lexi holds up the folder in her hand. "Grey asked me to bring by the lease transfer. He already signed it."

"Come on in, then." Mr. Peters holds open the door and we all go inside and head toward the kitchen.

"This should be quick and easy," Lexi explains when we reach the dining table. "Grey signed a one-year lease with Mr. Peters, but he's agreed to break it. We just need both your signatures to transfer it over."

"Thank you." I take the pen from her and bend over the pages, skimming over the terms of the lease. I sign where she indicates, and when I'm done, she hands the packet over to my grandfather.

While he's reviewing it, she turns to me, her head tilting to one side. "Have we met before?"

I startle. "No. I don't think so . . . but you do seem familiar."

Her brows dip in thought, and then she shakes her head. "But I'm sure we've never met. So weird."

Mr. Peters finishes signing off and hands Lexi the paperwork.

She puts it back in the folder. "Thanks. I'll get out of your way now. But, hey, Amelia, do you want to grab a drink or dinner or something next weekend?"

My eyes widen. "I would really love that."

"Yeah?" She grins and hands me some papers. "Here's a copy of the lease. My number's at the top. Give me a call once you get settled in."

"I will, absolutely." Surprise flickers through me, tinged with a vague sense of déjà vu.

I don't have time to analyze the sensations because once she's gone, we gather the rest of the boxes from the back of the truck before Mr. Peters has to leave as well.

"I don't want to wear you out or talk your ear off on your first day here. It's getting late and I'm sure you'll want to get settled."

"You don't have to go yet." He's right, I should get my stuff unpacked, but I don't want him to leave. The past week since his first call has been like some crazy fever dream and I'm worried I'll wake up and discover none of it is real.

"It's fine. I can let you get settled. We'll have plenty of time to get to know each other."

I nod. He's right. I'm not planning on going

anywhere. "I have to work in the mornings, but after that I'm free."

"You said you're a writer?"

"Yes. I've been doing freelance writing. It's not much, but I can do it from anywhere and it's enough to pay the bills."

"Well, that's just fine. It worked out well for us then."

"I think so, too. Thank you for letting me stay here."

"It's no trouble. I bought this house intending for it to stay in our family, and now it can. And having someone here helps me so I don't have to pay someone to maintain the property."

Before he goes, he shows me a whiteboard near the phone in the kitchen with his phone number and other emergency contacts.

"Oh, one more thing," he says when we're out on the porch. "There's a spare key, but my last tenant has it. He should be coming by here shortly." He glances at his watch.

"That's fine. Thank you again. I'll see you tomorrow."

I wait until his Cadillac disappears down the driveway before going back inside.

I'll see you tomorrow. Have there ever been any more glorious words?

"Bob," I call out. "We're home."

I head to the master bedroom where we set my suitcase and get to work unpacking my clothes.

Opening the closet door, I yank on the light and then gaze into the empty space. Déjà vu smacks me upside the head so hard, I see stars. I sink down to my knees, my eyes drawn to a board in the back.

It's like my arms no longer belong to my body, like they know exactly what to do and I'm just a witness as they reach forward and tug up the board, exposing a hole underneath.

I reach inside and pick up Polaroid photos.

The photographs are of a man and a woman and—my breath catches—it's me. I'm the woman in these photos, and the man—my throat closes. My heart pounds in my chest.

This is impossible.

In one picture, he's kissing my cheek. I flip to the next. Both of us, smiling at the camera. And then next, I'm sticking my tongue out and he's pursing his lips with his eyes crossed.

I reach back into the hole, like the explanation is somewhere inside, and pull out . . . a condom?

Faint knocking reaches my ears through the bewilderment surrounding me.

Someone's here.

In a daze, I walk out to the front door, one of the pictures and a condom still clutched in my hand.

I open the door.

It's him, the man from the photo.

He's smiling at me, his face warm and dear and oh so familiar. His eyes crinkle, brown and warm.

I look down at the picture and then back up at him.

His smile falters. "Are you okay? Amelia?" He clears his throat. "You're Amelia, right?" he says very seriously and I know he's lying. I know it like I know my own heartbeat.

I stare at him.

He steps into the house. "I'm Grey. I have the spare key for you. Did Gregory tell you I was coming by?"

It takes me a few long seconds to respond, to register his words. Blood is roaring in my ears. Pressure is building, like I'm in a plane, ascending, and my ears won't pop.

Finally, I nod.

He smiles and reaches out a hand, the movement casual, but there's a tightness to his shoulders and mouth, like he's anticipating something.

But how can I know this? Where are these thoughts coming from? How I could read this complete stranger that well? Because he's not a stranger. I know it. It's like I'm dreaming. Nothing feels real.

Hesitantly, I reach for him with my free hand.

His fingers engulf mine and I exhale into a rush of awareness.

Images flick through my mind, slowly at first, and then flooding me all at once. My knees give out.

Seeing Grey for the first time.

Kissing Grey for the first time.

Lexi.

Preston.

Claire.

Don.

Bob.

We're on the floor. I blink up into Grey's concerned face, only inches away. I've collapsed and now I'm sitting in his lap in the entryway.

His arms tighten when I open my eyes, a dent between his brows. "Are you okay?"

"Grey?"

When I say his name, my voice laced with awe and recognition, he smiles wide, his joy filling my vision, filling the room. "Do you remember?"

"I didn't until just now. Holy hell, that was awful. I have a headache."

He laughs. "You think that was awful. I had to wait over a month for you to get here and I remembered everything."

I grip his shoulders. "Grey." His name is an oath and a prayer.

Then his lips are on mine and the heat of his mouth has me melting, leaning into him, reveling in the fact that he's here, that I'm here, that we're here together and all of this is really happening.

His mouth travels from my mouth to my neck, peppering kisses, sucking on the delicate skin of my throat and I moan, heat already building.

"Grey."

"Hmmm?" He continues his path, tugging my shirt down to lick across my collarbone. "I want you." One of his hands leaves me, reaching for something on the floor. "It was excellent foresight for you to bring this to the door with you." He lifts the condom.

Laughter bubbles out of me and he immediately kisses my mouth, as if to taste the joy and humor on my lips.

I tug on his shirt and he whips it over his head. Then we're undressing each other with frantic, impatient hands, and he's ripping the condom package with his teeth and rolling the it on.

He rolls over, laying back on the hard floor and hauling me on top of him.

I don't want to wait. I can't wait. I sink down onto him without preamble and we both groan at the sensation.

He shifts under me, abs flexing as he curves up to kiss me, tug on my earlobe with his teeth, brush his lips over my shoulder, then my breast, his arms surrounding me.

I relish in the sensations, his warmth, his strength, his eyes glittering up at me.

"Amelia." His hips thrust up while I push down, riding him in complete abandon, my body burning and blazing.

His hand sneaks between our bodies, finding the place we're connected and rubbing, circling, until I come undone.

I call out his name, my body a writhing mass of pleasure as I slump over him.

His fingers dig into my hips and he jerks into me a few more times before his own release pulses inside me.

We lie on the entryway floor, collecting our breath.

Eventually, I lift my head from his chest to look into his face.

Grey pushes my hair out of the way and smiles at me. "Hi."

A smile spreads across my face, so wide my cheeks hurt. "Hi."

His hand cups my face, his eyes fixed on mine. "I love you, you know."

My heart swells, skips a beat, thunders and then rises up into my eyes, leaving them misty. "I love you, too."

His head lifts, kissing me on the lips, my cheek, my eye, then back to my lips.

Bob meows, prancing over to us from the hallway.

"We love you too, Bob," Grey tells her.

She flicks her tail, unimpressed, and then saunters off toward the kitchen.

"We have a lot to talk about."

I blow out a breath. "Once the postcoital haze clears, I'm sure I'll have some questions."

"Let's move this show somewhere a little more comfortable."

I tap Grey on the chest. "Do you want some food?"

"I thought you'd never ask."

We get partially dressed—Grey puts his boxers back on, and I throw on his T-shirt—and then we settle in the living room.

He releases me only to grab the tray of food from me and set it on the coffee table, and then we sit on the couch together and he wraps an arm around me, as if he needs to be touching me at all times.

It's so bizarre, a complete repeat from the past. I mean, the future.

"Where do you want to start?" he asks.

"So . . . my grandfather. Before, he didn't reach out to me after my parents died. And then I wrote that article. I haven't done that yet. I didn't get a chance to even consider it because he called me."

His smile is full of smug satisfaction. "I know. At first, I was going to try and find you, reach you, but I wasn't sure if you would remember me. I just knew I had to get you up here and out of your dark space." He rubs my arm. "I knew you needed your grandfather more than you needed some strange dude claiming to know you from some other time dimension."

I stare at him, wondering at this man, how he knows how to take care of me. "How did you get him to call me?"

"I knew he already wanted to. I told you he prayed for you. He cared. He worried when your parents died. He really just needed the smallest nudge. Oh, and your phone number."

I blink. "You gave him my number? How did you find it?" I know I'm not listed.

"I creeped on your phone and memorized it." He shrugs. "It was a bit of a gamble. I couldn't know how much I would remember, but I didn't forget anything. Just like I told you I wouldn't." He tugs me closer, and I move willingly, my cheek against his chest, breathing in his scent.

My mind is still recovering, trying to make sense of the two timelines, now irrevocably altered. I have so many questions, I don't even know where to start.

"What happened after you came out of the in-between place?"

He tugs me into his lap. "Sorry. I need you closer to me than I need to eat."

I beam at him. "I don't mind."

His arms tighten around me. "I woke up on the dining room floor, and Don was there next to me, knocked out. I called 9-1-1. I told them what had happened, what I remembered of it, which wasn't much beyond eating the pie and waking up with Don there. They tested Claire's pie and discovered that it had been laced with Ambien."

My hands clench against him. "I'm so grateful it wasn't something stronger."

"Me, too. She gave my mom something stronger."

"I'm sorry."

He takes a deep breath, squeezing me before continuing. "Turns out, Joe was going to leave her for my mom. I think Mom was going to tell me that weekend, that's why she wanted me to come into town to talk. But before that could happen, Claire killed her. Except, by then, Joe was suspicious."

I pull back to look at him. "But he stayed with her for three more years before he died."

He shrugs. "I can't explain it. I imagine Claire had convinced him she was a docile wife as we all believed her to be, but at some point, he must have decided to leave anyway. That's when Claire killed him by inducing a stroke."

I shudder. "I don't think I'm going to be able to eat pie ever again."

"Tell me about it."

"What about Don?"

"Obviously, Don helped her get rid of me—before. He was helping her the whole time."

I nod, thinking. "I bet he was that figure outside my house with the knife."

"That makes sense."

"Why was he helping her?"

He considers the question. "I bet she was paying him or something. And clearly, they had some sort of relationship. He must know he's Preston's father. Maybe she used his relationship with Preston to convince him."

"Or blackmail him."

He nods. "Who knows? She isn't saying much. Her and Don are both awaiting trial. I wonder how much more will come out then."

We hold each other for a few long minutes, mired in grim thoughts.

"What about Preston?" I ask.

"He isn't talking. I think he might have known or

had some suspicions, but didn't want to believe it. He might have been trying to protect her. I've been trying to reach him, connect with him, but he hasn't left his house since all this came out and he's not returning my calls."

It's kind of sad. "I wonder if he knew when you were kids, if he found out you were Joe's son, and that's why he was mean, why he changed."

"It's definitely possible."

I lean back in his lap to meet his eyes. "So now what?"

"What do you mean?"

"I mean, how are we going to explain all this?"

His head tilts. "What is there to explain?"

"How—by all appearances—we just met today and now we're like, a couple in love?"

He grins and kisses my neck.

I sigh heavily. "People are going to think we're nuts."

"I don't care what people think as long as we're together. Like Rick Astley, I'm never gonna give you up."

I laugh, shoving him in the shoulder, and then we're kissing again.

"Amelia." His forehead touches mine, his breath feathering my lips. "Welcome home."

The End

Fox Family Series

Between a Fox and a Hard Place

The Fox and the Rebound

Another Fox Bites the Dust

Some Like It Fox

For Fox Sake

About the Author

Go here to sign up for the newsletter!
www.maryframe.com

Mary Frame is a full-time mother and wife with a full-time job. She has no idea how she manages to write novels except that it helps being a dedicated introvert. She doesn't enjoy writing about herself in third person, but she does enjoy reading, writing, dancing, and damaging the eardrums of her coworkers when she randomly decides to sing to them. She lives in Reno, Nevada, with her husband, two children, and a border collie named Stella.

She LOVES hearing from readers and will not only respond but likely begin stalking them while tossing out hearts and flowers and rainbows! If that doesn't creep you out, email her at:
maryframeauthor@gmail.com